Before Elizabeth

the story of Anne de Bourgh

Rohase Piercy

This is a work of fiction. Any resemblance to persons living or dead is purely coincidental.

Before Elizabeth
Copyright © 2017 Rohase Piercy
All rights reserved.

No part of this text may be used or reproduced in any form, except for the inclusion of brief quotations in review, without written permission from the author.

Cover Design by Basil Chap

ISBN: 1539868214

ISBN-13: 978-1539868217

BEFORE ELIZABETH

*For Morgana and Pip,
who grew up with this story.*

*****chapter one*****

It is a truth universally acknowledged that I have inherited little in terms of character, and even less as to looks, from my mother's side of the family – universally, because even Mama, having searched in vain for my features amongst two centuries of Fitzwilliam family portraits, has herself been forced to acknowledge it. She comforts herself with the reflection that in my plain, pale countenance and unimpressive figure resides the august history of my father's family, now sadly diminished; the family into which she married with such hopes of conjugal felicity and consequence two years before my birth; the family de Bourgh.

We are of French origin, and my father and grandfather were anxious to maintain the connection at a time when no-one had yet heard the name 'Buonaparte'. It is my father's sister, Lady Isabelle, whom I am said most to resemble - indeed I would have been named for her, had not my mother demanded that her own sister's name take precedence. Her insistence carried the day and I was baptised Anne Isabel de Bourgh, in the little parish church of Hunsford, shortly after my birth in the year 1791. My Aunt Isabelle was not present; she had lately married a French cousin possessed of a fine estate on the outskirts of Paris, thus making her the envy of all the young women of Kent. And so I was destined never to set eyes upon her, for in my third year both she and her husband met their deaths by guillotine under Robespierre's Terror. Like many others they had thought themselves invincible, dismissing the concerns of their English relatives and delaying their departure from France until it was too late. My grandfather outlived his daughter by less than a year, blaming himself to the end for having encouraged the French marriage.

There is a portrait in the long gallery at Rosings which held a particular fascination for me as a child. It shows my father as a young boy, bewigged and powdered for the occasion, standing stiffly to attention at my grandfather's knee, his blue eyes betraying even then that look of mild apprehension which I remember so well. His sister, my young aunt, stands encircled by her mother's arm, equally pale and solemn in stiff blue satins with a Cavalier spaniel at her feet. She is the only member of the group whose eye seems to meet that of the beholder, and to my young self it was like looking at my own reflection in the glass, in spite of the uncomfortable satin and powdered ringlets; for it is true - I do resemble her, in almost every feature. And my father, who had loved his sister dearly, doted upon the daughter who favoured her so closely and was as lavish in his indulgence of me as Mama was lavish in her disappointment. I was their only child, and she had hoped for a son.

It is a question worth asking: why did my parents

marry? Why would a man of Papa's temperament - given the choice as he undoubtedly was of so many young ladies of fortune - choose Lady Catherine Fitzwilliam, probably the least likely to contribute to his domestic happiness? Did it really mean so much to him, to secure the daughter of an Earl? Physically she was quite his opposite, tall and queenly as her bearing still is, with dark eyes and strong features; and as to character - perhaps it was her very air of assurance which attracted him? Perhaps he believed that with her at his side, the social duties required of his situation would be less taxing to his shy and gentle nature. One does hear of such matches, and sometimes they are very successful - but not, alas, in my parents' case.

And my mother? What could have attracted the Earl of Amberleigh's daughter to a mere baronet, and a quiet and unassuming one at that? Ah, that is easy! In those days as in these a noble name did not of itself secure an income, and the Fitzwilliam daughters could not afford to marry without some attention to their future material comfort. My father was heir not only to a baronetcy, but also to a large, well-managed estate whose revenue was secure. Careless, at that stage, of what disappointments his character might hold for her upon closer acquaintance, Lady Catherine Fitzwilliam would have needed very little persuasion to look favourably upon Lewis de Bourgh's proposal.

Old Sir Lewis, so the story goes, was initially uneasy; he was a wise and protective father, and knew his son well. But it was an eligible match; the Earl of Amberleigh had given his consent; and perhaps it was in my grandfather's mind that so strong a young woman would bring robust blood into the family, enhancing its health along with its nobility. The arrangements were duly made, and the wedding invitations dispatched.

Chief among the guests in my mother's eyes must surely have been her younger sister, Lady Anne, who had entered the marriage state some seven years earlier. She had married for love, and her husband, although wealthy and in possession of a fine estate in Derbyshire, was distinguished by no other title than that of *Mr.* How Mama must have relished having her restoration to seniority as wife of the future Sir Lewis de Bourgh and mistress of Rosings Park witnessed by Mr and Mrs Darcy of Pemberley, and their six-year-old son and heir!

She was confident, of course, that she also would produce a son in due course. When I arrived she hid her disappointment as best she could, and as the likelihood of my being joined by a brother diminished with each ensuing year she consoled herself by arranging, in her own mind at least, a match between her daughter and her sister's only son - between myself and my cousin, Fitzwilliam Darcy.

Fitzwilliam Darcy - known in the family circle as William. There, I have done it. I have forced my pen to write his name.

*****chapter two*****

I was about four years old when my father came into his inheritance. The shocking events that had taken place in France the year before had been kept from me, and the death of my grandfather, old Sir Lewis, made no deep impression upon me since the old man had been a partial invalid and I had seen him but little. My most vivid memory of that time is of the noise of hammering and sawing, the smell of wood shavings and linseed oil, and the loud, coarse voices of the workmen requisitioned by my father to carry out a necessary program of improvement and modernisation to Rosings Park. The transformation of my home around me held a natural fascination, and provided Mrs Jenkinson accompanied me I was allowed to observe the work in progress, at a safe distance, whenever I liked.

Mrs Jenkinson had been Aunt Isabelle's governess. She was a great favourite with old Sir Lewis, whose affection for her survived her desertion from the household in order to marry an attorney from Rochester, and secured her a warm welcome back to Rosings upon her Mr Jenkinson's untimely death. Since I was but a baby then, she was given the position of unofficial assistant to the housekeeper until I should be old enough to need a governess; and the fact that Mrs Henderson found no reason to complain of this arrangement is testament enough to Mrs Jenkinson's tactful qualities.

It was not until after my seventh birthday that she was requisitioned to superintend my education; and a very gentle and easy education it was, much to Mama's disapproval. Knowing the affectionate regard in which my father held such a loyal family retainer, she did not at first express this disapproval directly; but when her pejorative hints had fallen upon deaf ears for nigh on two years, the limit of her tolerance was reached.

"How you can possibly continue to entrust your daughter's education to that idle, uninformed old creature is beyond my comprehension! She has no business to be superintending a young lady's education at her time of life - she has neither the stamina nor the intellect. Her knowledge of modern languages, history and world affairs is woefully inadequate. A little music, a little needlework, that is all she is fit to teach our daughter!"

Tiptoeing past the half-open door of the library, I froze, appalled.

"Isabelle received a perfectly adequate schooling from Mrs Jenkinson. My father engaged masters to supplement her education where necessary, and we can do the same for Anne." Papa's voice was quiet but clipped - she had made him angry. I imagined his lips pressed tightly together, his hands folded upon the desk before him. Mama blundered on, oblivious.

"Our daughter is the Heiress of Rosings! She

requires a modern education, not the sort of romantic nonsense that filled your sister's head. No doubt Isabelle was thought very accomplished in her day -"

"She was indeed thought so. She was one of the most accomplished young ladies in the country, the intelligence of her mind equaled only by the sweetness of her nature. If you intend to speak ill of my sister this conversation is at an end, Catherine."

I caught my breath, having seldom heard my father speak so forcefully; Mama was likewise taken aback, and momentarily silenced.

"Nevertheless," he continued wearily, "it may be true that Mrs Jenkinson has not the stamina to apply herself as once she did. I shall speak to her, and if she agrees, an assistant can be engaged for the tuition of those subjects to which she may feel herself unequal. It is of Mrs Jenkinson's wellbeing that I am thinking," he concluded firmly, lest Mama should think that her insistence had carried the day; and she, having won her case, was content to allow him the last word.

It was at this point that Mrs Jenkinson herself appeared on the landing above, and I launched myself up the staircase to reach her, sacrificing silence to speed. My mother was at the door in an instant.

"Anne? Anne! Whatever are you doing, child, clattering up the stairs like that? Have I not told you a hundred times that a lady does not run? Ah, is that Mrs Jenkinson? Come down Mrs Jenkinson, if you please, and be so good as to step into the library. Sir

Lewis wishes to speak to you."

Before she could obey, I had reached the top of the stairs and threw my arms about her waist. I felt her palm, soft and puckered like embroidered satin against my cheek, and as she gently disengaged herself I seized her hand and kissed it, whispering fiercely, "I shall always love you best, Jenky. I promise I shall always love you best!"

How fickle is the heart of a spoiled child! Miss Harvey arrived at Rosings less than a fortnight later, and as soon as I set eyes upon her I was smitten. Miss Harvey's history, as related by herself, was a most romantic one: her father, a Lieutenant of Marines, had been killed in action abroad whilst gallantly saving the life of his Captain. Upon hearing the sad news, her mother - a gentlewoman of unspecified family who had braved parental disapproval to marry for love - had fallen into a decline from which she never recovered, leaving her little daughter dependent upon the kindness of an uncle. This excellent man had received his niece into his family upon her mother's death, and brought her up at his own expense. He could not provide an independent income for her however, and so she was obliged, at the age of nineteen, to seek a suitable situation. And now she stood before us, a tall, confident young woman with an abundance of red curls, sly green eyes, a pretty tilted nose and a coquettish smile.

"This is your first situation, is it not?" Mama's

voice and expression were eloquent of disapproval; her eyes were upon the elaborate ringlets. I sat upon my low stool, my folded hands clenched in anguish, wishing that someone had warned this beautiful creature about my mother's opinions on coiffure.

"Yes indeed, Your Ladyship. My uncle is most anxious to see me well placed out, and insists that I apply only to the best families."

"Does he." Mama glanced briefly at the letter in her hand. "He naturally speaks highly of you, but whether you will meet the standards of Sir Lewis de Bourgh remains to be seen. You have traveled abroad, I understand?"

"Yes, ma'am, I have visited both Italy and France."

"Indeed! Captain Fairchild has been most liberal - I hope you have not been brought up too high, and encouraged to think yourself above your station in life."

A heightened colour was discernible upon Miss Harvey's cheek as she answered with equanimity, "Indeed not, Your Ladyship. I am only grateful that my uncle's liberality has equipped me to be useful."

Her green gaze slid momentarily towards me. There was an expression in her eyes that I could not decipher. Mama made a sharp movement, both annoyed and conciliatory. "Your French is fluent then, I presume?"

"Mais oui, bien sur Madame. J'ai etudié la langue avec grand plaisir."

Her accent was good, and Mama was impressed.

"And your knowledge of literature, of history ancient and modern?"

"Is perfectly adequate, I do assure you ma'am. I had the advantage of some excellent masters."

"H'mm." She raised her lorgnette and studied the letter for several minutes, while Miss Harvey made a leisurely perusal of our drawing room, avoiding my rapt gaze. At length Mama said abruptly, without raising her eyes from the letter, "You will not be required to teach needlework. That is Mrs Jenkinson's responsibility. Drawing and dancing lessons will also be taken care of in due course." She lowered her lorgnette and surveyed her candidate coolly. "Tell me, Miss Harvey, do you play and sing?"

"I do, Your Ladyship."

"H'mm. That is not always suitable in a governess. However, if Mrs Jenkinson is agreeable, you may oversee my daughter in practicing her instrument. Mrs Jenkinson has not the time to attend to it as often as I would like, and I am sure you will agree with me that constant practice is the only path to proficiency upon the pianoforte."

And with that, she reached for the bell, gesturing Miss Harvey towards the door.

"You will make your arrangements with your guardian, and I shall send a carriage for you at ten on Friday. I trust that will give you sufficient time to prepare?"

Miss Harvey's features relaxed visibly as she gave her assent and expressed her gratitude. As she turned to leave, she slid me another glance; this time there was no mistaking the mockery in those green eyes.

If my father had expected Mama to refer to him in the matter of Miss Harvey's appointment he showed little surprise, and no opposition. She duly arrived, was installed in the schoolroom, and set about the task of supplementing my education in a most thrilling manner. Along with French and Modern History I learned a great deal that would have horrified Mama had she known of it! Considering her objections to 'romantic nonsense', she had certainly made a singular choice of governess; gossip and scandal were meat and drink to Miss Harvey, and she could not have indulged her predilection upon a more attentive pupil.

Soon I knew all about the last great days of the French court, the Queen's intrigues and the King's excesses, the onset of the Terror and the horrors of the guillotine which sent noble heads toppling into the basket below with lips still quivering. I awoke screaming in the night, and had to be soothed with possets by Mrs Jenkinson, whom I observed in quiet conversation with Miss Harvey on the following day. She, sullenly aware of Mrs Jenkinson's senior position in the household, announced to me later in the schoolroom that she would speak no more of 'those sad events in France in which your dear Aunt met her untimely fate'. Instead, she would speak of our own Royal Family, beloved and cherished by their subjects here in this Sceptered Isle where such horrors as the French had brought down upon themselves could never, ever occur.

And so I learned of the secret marriage of the Prince of Wales to Mrs Maria Fitzherbert, which was, said Miss Harvey, no secret at all, no more than was his disgust for the vulgar German habits of his official wife the Princess Caroline, whom he could scarcely bear to have near him. This information gave me no nightmares, but it did prompt me to seek Mrs Jenkinson's opinion of the whole sorry business as she superintended my supper one evening.

She regarded me with careful alarm. "Of whom are you speaking, my dear?"

"Of Mrs Fitzherbert," I replied innocently, swallowing a mouthful of bread and butter. "Miss Harvey says that everyone knows she is the Prince's true wife, and that his marriage to the Princess Caroline is but a sham. He only married her so they could have the Princess Charlotte, and now he cannot bear the sight of her. So Miss Harvey says Mrs Fitzherbert need have no worries in that quarter but must keep a sharp eye on that brazen hussy Lady Jersey!"

Mrs Jenkinson's teacup made a rapid descent to her saucer. "Miss Harvey has no business to be telling you such things! If that is her idea of Modern History then I think that your parents should be informed."

I was horrified, not having anticipated such disapproval; tears of mortification sprang to my eyes. "Oh Jenky, no! Please don't tell Mama! Miss

Harvey means no harm - she says that current events are history in the making, and it all goes to show that human nature does not change."

Mrs Jenkinson could not suppress a smile. "Oh, does she? Well, there is truth in that, I will admit. But you must remember, my chicken, that Miss Harvey is still young and high-spirited; not all of her opinions are balanced ones, however interesting they may seem. Do you not think, for example, that the Princess of Wales must be very unhappy not to have the love of her husband? After all, she had even less choice in the marriage than he. And what of poor little Princess Charlotte? How must she feel, do you suppose, knowing her parents to be at war with one another, and the subject of common gossip to boot?"

I gave these matters some thought. "I suppose," I answered slowly, "it must be very unpleasant to marry someone who does not love you. But the Prince dotes upon the Princess Charlotte, Miss Harvey says. She is his only child, just as I am Papa's. That can't be so bad, no matter what people say."

Mrs Jenkinson got up and rang for the maid. "I think perhaps - have you cleared your plate? Good girl - I think there is no need to trouble your mother, but perhaps your *father* should have a quiet word with Miss Harvey."

Kind, wise Mrs Jenkinson! In approaching Papa, she was able to balance her concern for my moral welfare with her wish to see me happy, and secure all for the best. He sent for me from his library on the following afternoon, and when, full of trepidation, I tiptoed into that green-carpeted room where fingers of sunlight reached through the long windows to make a leisurely exploration of the book-lined shelves, I found him smiling, his mild blue eyes full of amusement.

"Come in, my dear. Come and sit down." He motioned me towards the stiff, uncomfortable sofa where he joined me, having carefully marked the place in his book and laid it down upon the desk.

"I hear that Miss Harvey has been telling you some exciting stories, and not only of the fairy-tale variety," he began kindly, patting my knee in a playful manner as I wriggled against the unyielding upholstery. "Mrs Fitzherbert and Lady Jersey! Well, well. All very instructive and entertaining I'm sure, but not quite what your mother would expect your lessons to consist of. And stories from France which are perhaps not appropriate at a time when that great nation is posing so real a threat to our gallant navy. The diamond necklace of Queen Marie-Antoinette may be a very romantic tale, but the reality today is the necklace of conquests with which Admiral Buonaparte seeks to adorn his mother country! But take heart, Anne - I would not have your education consist solely of dry and gloomy texts. I have suggested to Miss Harvey that she make her romantic forays into the world of literature and poetry, where you will find much to please you both, I think. There is much more to literature than Dr Johnson's opinions and Fordyce's sermons! For intrigue, what say you to the novels of Miss Fanny Burney, or even, since your interest in human nature has obviously been awakened, to those of Mr Fielding? For romance, why not linger amongst the sonnets of Shakespeare, or the latest outpourings of Mr Wordsworth? I have told Miss Harvey that she is to come to the library every week and choose books which you may read together, subject to my approval. And you must tell me which authors are most to your liking, that I may direct her choice accordingly. Shall you like that?"

And so my solitary education gathered pace. Miss Harvey and I dallied amongst the raptures of Cowper and Wordsworth and thrilled to the perils of 'Tom Jones' and 'Tristram Shandy', and Papa took pleasure in my growing appreciation of his library, and the cultivation of my literary taste. I also made tolerable progress in French and Italian, could name all the capital cities and principal rivers of Europe, and embroidered a colourful fire screen for the schoolroom. Only mastery of music seemed destined to elude me. I would much rather listen to Miss Harvey play and sing (which she did with much sentiment and flourish, an exciting contrast to the gentle warblings of Mrs Jenkinson) than practice my instrument; and she was quite happy to oblige me in this.

As for my mother, who made it her business to inquire into every detail of her household's activity, and who had expressed such meticulous concern over my education - she appeared to have no qualms about Miss Harvey whatsoever. Assuring all who would listen that my governess found my aptitude second to none, my progress outstanding and my understanding exceptional, she congratulated herself on having selected so perceptive an instructress to guide me. Under Miss Harvey's superintendence, she confidently declared, I was set to become one of the most accomplished young women in the country.

*****chapter three*****

Having secured her employer's good opinion along with her pupil's affection, and perceiving her position in the schoolroom to be junior to Mrs Jenkinson in name only, Miss Harvey soon came to consider herself an established member of the household. When Mama announced that her brother, the Earl of Amberleigh, would shortly be making his usual Easter visit with his two grown-up sons, she could scarcely contain her excitement and began to quiz me eagerly about my Fitzwilliam relatives. I was more than happy to oblige her, especially when it came to Edward, my uncle's younger son and my favourite cousin. Although well into his twenties and preparing to take up a commission in the Army, Edward always showed me the kindest attention during his visits to Rosings, listening to my news and answering my questions with the utmost seriousness. His elder brother John by contrast hardly noticed me except to tease; the heir to the Amberleigh estate found the limited society of Hunsford tedious, and was often absent from the family circle altogether, lured away by the proximity of London. As for my uncle, he was a man of uncertain temper, afflicted by gout, who had lost all incentive to make himself agreeable in company with the death of his wife some years ago. He made little effort to converse with my father, and for his part Papa seemed quite happy to let his wife entertain her brother and eldest nephew while he spent his time with Edward, whose company he clearly preferred. They would make tours of the Park together and spend hours locked away in the library, much to Mama's annoyance. For my part, I rejoiced in the friendship between my beloved father and my favourite cousin, knowing myself secure in the affections of both.

Miss Harvey, however, took a startlingly different view of the matter. "Well, Sir Lewis has no male heir, has he? 'Tis only to be expected that he will favour one of his nephews. No wonder your poor mother finds his partiality irksome - 'twill serve only to remind her of his failure!"

"His failure? Miss Harvey, what can you mean?" I asked, astonished.

"Why, his failure to father a son, of course!" she responded tartly; and seeing my shocked expression, added "Well, he fathered you, did he not? He could surely have tried just once more!"

I understood her just well enough not to wish for further clarification. Outraged, I sprang to Papa's defence.

"I don't think it is your place to speak so of my father, Miss Harvey. And in any case, my parents do not need a son, because they have me. *I* am the heiress of Rosings."

Miss Harvey laughed, but not pleasantly. "Oh, well said, Miss Anne. Aren't we the grand young lady when we want to be! Quite the little Princess

Charlotte. Well then, what do you think of this: there's talk below stairs of your father adopting Mr Edward Fitzwilliam as his son and heir. *Now* what have you to say?"

As soon as I recovered the power of speech, I had a great deal to say. I hotly denied the possibility of any such thing, demanding to know from whom she had heard such a wicked lie, and threatening to go straight to Papa to demand that the slander be refuted, and the culprit exposed. Realising that she had gone too far, Miss Harvey hastily assured me that it was but an idle rumor, arising no doubt from some stable hand with no real knowledge of the household; that there was no need to distress my father by repeating such tittle-tattle, and that she herself did not believe a word of it. She moved swiftly onto safer ground, and began heartily to endorse my low opinion of my cousin John; Mr Fitzwilliam, she said, was reckoned by the servants to be a great coxcomb, idle and vain, and 'a danger to the female sex' - not one of them had a good word to say for him.

I allowed myself to be mollified, but her words had done their damage. I became more and more preoccupied by the relationship between Papa and Edward. It was not only here at Rosings that they spent time together – I knew that they met frequently in London and had only last summer made a trip to Brighton, a place Mama refused to visit on account of the vulgarity of its boarding houses. Might there not after all be a grain of truth in the 'idle gossip' which Miss Harvey had so recklessly imparted and then so hastily denied? I resisted the temptation to confide in Mrs Jenkinson, as I feared that the consequences would be catastrophic for Miss Harvey and humiliating for me. I decided instead to make my own observations, and see what information I could glean from them.

Edward's affectionate greeting and easy manner towards me upon his arrival did much to dispel my worries; his smile was as kind as ever, the sweet expression in his light brown eyes a welcome contrast to the dark brooding stares of my older cousin and uncle. As the days progressed I watched him closely, paying particular attention to his manner towards Papa: was it really that of a prospective son and heir? I did not think so: there was nothing of paternal authority in Papa's manner, or of filial acquiescence in Edward's. It was surely a friendship between equals, pure and simple. But I had to be certain, and one afternoon when my lessons were over I boldly requisitioned my cousin's company for the task of gathering daffodils to decorate the schoolroom. As we strolled hand in hand across the lawn towards the green shade of the cedars, where a veritable carpet of cream and yellow blooms danced invitingly, I began clumsily to quiz him about his expectations: where would he live when he received his commission? Would he take a house in town? When John became Lord Amberleigh and inherited Evesham House, would he still be able to live there?

If not, where would he go? &c.

At first, Edward seemed amused by my questions. "Why, Anne, what is all this? Are you so concerned for my future? I shall not be an Ensign for long, you know; thanks to my father I can expect a rapid promotion, and in a year or so I shall be a Captain, with a hundred men under my command! And a Captain, you know, must be with his battalion for most of the time. But I shall always have a home at Evesham, I expect, unless my brother marries someone who takes a dislike to me; and yes, I shall probably take a house in town eventually. Why so serious, little cousin? I shall always come often to Kent, to visit my uncle and to assure myself that the heiress of Rosings is still the most beautiful and accomplished young lady in the country. Will that do?"

The phrase 'heiress of Rosings' was not lost upon me. I nodded and smiled, but persisted in my questioning: "Will you not need an estate of your own though, Edward, when you are married?"

My cousin knelt down amongst the daffodils and began to select blooms at random, suddenly preoccupied. At length he repeated, "An estate of my own! Well, I do not know about that. I shall do well enough for a younger son, I dare say; I'm sure plenty of people will advise me to marry a rich heiress, and acquire a grand house in that way. But as I said, I am to be a soldier. That is the life I have decided upon, and it will suit me well enough for the foreseeable future. I may choose not to marry at all; what do you think of that?"

I did now know what to think of it. "I thought everyone had to be married," I said, heedlessly crushing the hem of my gown into the dirt as I sat back on my heels to consider the matter.

Edward laughed. "Well, it is not yet enshrined in English law! It is the general expectation, I suppose, and maybe in due course I shall give it some thought. But not yet, and certainly not now, on such a beautiful spring day when the Park is dancing with daffodils! Come now, cousin, you are not keeping to your part of the bargain - I have a fine armful of blooms already, and what have you? Nothing! You must match me stem for stem, and we will carry them back to the house and ask Mrs Jenkinson to bring us two great vases. Then we shall have a display to do justice to Mr Wordsworth! My uncle tells me you have been enjoying his poetry - will you read to me while I am here? I should dearly love to hear you."

As we wandered back happily towards the house with our saffron bundles, I determined to set Miss Harvey right at the earliest opportunity. The only design that my cousin had upon Rosings was to visit often, and assure himself that its heiress - that was I - was still the most beautiful and accomplished young lady in the country! I searched for her later that afternoon, but failing to find her I returned to the schoolroom to daydream amongst the daffodils, imagining a dozen pleasant future scenarios involving Edward, my father and my grown-up self before hitting upon the one that so obviously suited every convenience and solved every problem that I leapt to my feet, transported by the genius of my own imagination!

What was it that had Edward said? *'I'm sure plenty of people will advise me to marry a rich heiress, and acquire a grand house in that way.'* Well, *I* would be a rich heiress - why should he not marry *me* in due course, and come to live at Rosings? Unable to remain still, I began to dance about the room as the possibility took root in my imagination and began to put forth shoots. What if this had been Papa's plan all along? Would not that explain everything, from his special treatment of Edward to my cousin's embarrassment when I brought up the subject of marriage? Oh, what to do – should I speak to Papa immediately, or wait until the Fitzwilliams had left us? Mrs Jenkinson would certainly advise me to wait... but Miss Harvey ...

Determined to find her there and then, I rushed headlong out onto the stairway, where I almost collided with Mrs Jenkinson coming to fetch me for supper.

"Oh Jenky!" I gasped, ignoring her gentle admonition, "Do you know where Miss Harvey is? I've been looking for her everywhere!"

"She is out walking," was her cool reply, in tones so laced with disapproval that my curiosity was aroused.

"Out walking where?" I demanded, as she ushered me firmly along the corridor towards the nursery –

and then, as an unmistakable peal of laughter rose up the stairwell towards us, I ducked out from her restraining grasp and rushed to the banister just in time to see my governess enter the hallway on the arm of my cousin John! Disengaging herself from his eager grasp, she removed her bonnet and re-arranged a stray curl; and as he pulled playfully upon her arm, Mrs Jenkinson pulled firmly upon mine, telling me not to tarry as my soup was cooling. Dumbly I followed her, unable to make sense of the scene I had just witnessed - for had not Miss Harvey described John, in tones heavy with contempt, as a 'great coxcomb' and 'a danger to the female sex'? Why then would she walk with him, laugh with him, even – there was no other word for it – *flirt* with him in so obvious a manner? I had never seen her behave so, and it troubled me deeply. Upon reaching the nursery, I went straight to the table and ate my supper in silence - a silence upon which Mrs Jenkinson did not intrude, though she regarded me with watchful eyes.

John remained at Rosings until after Easter, giving me ample opportunity to observe the flirtation that he and Miss Harvey pursued whenever they thought themselves unobserved. They were discreet enough to escape the notice of my parents and uncle, but not that of the servants, whose barely concealed disapproval caused me agonies of mortification. It distressed me beyond words to see my beloved governess reduced to a simpering ninny by a man I so much disliked, and whose attentions she could surely not imagine to be serious. Could she not see that she was being made a fool of? When John left for London, abruptly and with no word of farewell to anyone save my mother, I breathed a long sigh of relief.

Miss Harvey's red eyes on the following morning, however, could not but arouse my pity. In an attempt to raise her spirits - and also to divert her attention towards a more deserving object - I invited her to join me in reading poetry with Edward that afternoon, a pastime which had already given me much pleasure. She looked at me as though I were utterly mad.

"What a baby you are, Miss Anne," she sniffed, tossing her red curls. "'Tis as well I set little store by *your* judgment of the male sex. Go and read to Mr Edward by all means, but don't expect me to hold your hand – not that you'll need a chaperone in *his* company!"

My pity evaporated upon the spot, and I retaliated in kind: "Just because my cousin John has made a fool of you in front of the whole household, 'tis no reason to take it out on me! And you were utterly wrong, you know, about Edward - Papa has no intention of adopting him."

I saw her fist clench, and knew that she would have struck me had she dared. Her face contorted into a sneer. "Well, I can see *that*!" she snapped; "I was wide of the mark *there*, and no mistake. That will teach me to listen to peasants' gossip! No wonder your poor mother complains - the sooner that young man goes into the Army, or gets married off to some poor undemanding fool, the better!"

At the mention of marriage I blushed involuntarily, and my cheeks burned hotter as Miss Harvey stared at me. Suddenly she began to laugh.

"Oh Lord! I don't believe it! You think you're to marry Mr Edward, don't you? You poor little fool! Well I've news for you Miss Anne, 'tis another cousin who's in line for you - young Mr Darcy, your mother's sister's son! What do you think of that? And you'd better raise your expectations before the wedding or you'll be in for a shock!"

I felt the blood drain from my face, leaving me as pale as I had been scarlet the moment before. "Young – young Mr Darcy?" I stammered, as William's stern, aquiline features and haughty expression leapt into my mind.

Miss Harvey laughed on, enjoying my discomfiture. "Don't tell me you had not an idea of it? Why, your mother is quite determined upon it, 'tis the talk of the household! He's quite the young gentleman, I hear, and handsome to boot – I'm sure I wish you joy. I'd settle myself for a husband half so fine!"

I left her still laughing as I ran from the schoolroom, heading for the sanctuary of the nursery where I could be alone. Closing the door behind me, I threw myself down upon the bed, burying my face in the bolster as the hot tears spilled.

In less than three months' time we would be

making our annual summer visit to Pemberley, which William's brooding presence and disapproving frown would no doubt once more drain of all enjoyment. It was always the same: my aunt and uncle would welcome me affectionately and do their best to put me at my ease, but all of their efforts would be brought to naught by their son's unsmiling, rigid manner. Whilst remaining perfectly polite, he would make it clear that he found my presence an irksome nuisance to be borne only at his parents' behest; he would dutifully chaperone me and my cousin Georgiana on all outdoor excursions, observing our play with haughty composure whilst refusing all invitations to participate; he would converse with me only when strictly necessary, in tones designed to reduce me to painful confusion. The possibility that this arrogant young man could be my future husband had never in my wildest dreams occurred to me. Was I to be sent away from Kent into the rugged wilds of Derbyshire? Was I actually to leave Rosings - my inheritance, my home – behind, and become the lifelong companion of someone whose society I dreaded? *Did Papa know of this?* Could this possibly have his approval?

With a few careless words Miss Harvey had rocked my world to its foundations, and now everything, everything was changed.

***** chapter four *****

My Uncle Fitzwilliam and Edward stayed only a week at Rosings following John's departure, and when they too had left us we found ourselves dull indeed. Mama declared herself bereft without her brother's company and complained that my father was but a poor substitute; Papa no doubt mirrored the sentiment privately, with regard to Edward. Miss Harvey was out of sorts with everyone, and I still in turmoil over her latest revelation, which I could not bring myself to confide to a living soul.

Could it really be, I asked myself repeatedly, that my parents expected me to *marry William?* Although, as I had said to Edward, I assumed matrimony to be everyone's inevitable fate, I had scarcely given a thought to my own prospects in that sphere until three weeks ago. Now, of course, I could think of little else. The comfortable continuation of life at Rosings with Edward and Papa which I had so fondly conjured up in my imagination had burst on the air like a bubble, and my chances of finding happiness in marriage now seemed slim indeed! After three days, I could bear it no more. I resolved to apply directly to Papa, confiding my distress and trusting in his honesty and kindness. Miss Harvey had been so cross with me lately that the fear of causing her trouble weighed little against the need to rid myself of so great a burden of uncertainty.

Papa replied immediately to my timid knock at the library door, bidding me enter and smiling encouragingly as he laid aside the letter he was writing. He drew up an extra chair to his great mahogany desk, watched patiently as I settled myself upon it, and then turned his own chair towards me, observing mildly, "You look serious, Anne. What can have brought you in all this state to visit me? It must be a weighty matter. You shall have my full attention."

I sat nervously twisting my fingers as he seated himself expectantly. "Come, come child, why so apprehensive? Out with it now – what troubles you?"

"Miss Harvey says that I am to marry William!" I blurted out at last, "And I do not know whether I shall like to, or why no-one has told me of it before!"

Papa's eyes widened briefly in surprise and displeasure. "Oh, Miss Harvey says that, does she? Miss Harvey is a great deal too free with her information, as usual."

His jaw clenched; for a few seconds his expression betrayed nothing but anger, and I began to feel afraid. But then he sighed, and adjusting his position in the chair leaned gently towards me and addressed me quietly and seriously.

"I am sorry that you have been distressed, Anne, over something that was never intended to be fearful to you. It is true that your Mama and your Aunt Darcy have discussed the possibility that one day you and your cousin may like one another enough to marry; it would be a tidy and suitable arrangement for both families. But there is no question of either of you being forced to it, if your inclinations are opposed. We are not Royalty, thank Heaven, and prospective marriages are not written in stone in these enlightened times! No-one is going to pressure you into a marriage you do not want Anne; you have my word upon it."

"Not Mama?" I ventured, frowning; and Papa smiled in rueful understanding as he smoothed my wrinkled brow with his forefinger.

"Not Mama. She may be a little disappointed if you choose elsewhere, but what matter? 'Tis our daughter's happiness that is important. The heiress of Rosings shall marry whom she wishes, within reason of course – you may refer to me in the matter if anyone dares say otherwise! But all the same, Anne, you may find that you come to like your cousin more as you both grow older. Let us wait and see, shall we?"

His assurances did much to comfort me; I ventured a smile, which was readily returned. Encouraged, I decided to press further.

"But Papa," I said bravely, "I like Edward much better than William, and you like him too; could I not marry Edward instead?"

My father placed his fingertips together thoughtfully, glancing across at the half-finished letter upon the desk. "Ah," he said carefully, "You think you would prefer to marry Edward. Well, well.

But you know, Anne, we often express preferences as children that we then review as adults – Edward is to be a soldier, you know, and often from home. You would not wish to have a husband who was often from home?"

Dimly aware that I was being fobbed off, I persisted recklessly: "But if I married Edward, I could stay here at Rosings, and not have to go away to Derbyshire! And when he had to go and fight the French I could keep you company, Papa – would not that be a much pleasanter arrangement?"

My father passed an agitated hand across his brow and replied, no doubt more sharply than he intended, "No my dear, it would not be a pleasant arrangement, and I must ask you to believe that on trust, for you are too young to understand the reasons for it. Let us leave all this talk of marriage now – it is too great a subject for a child of your age. I have given you all the reassurance in my power: you are under no obligation to marry your cousin William if you do not wish to. Let us leave it at that."

I felt a surge of panic rise in my breast, as the suspicions planted there by Miss Harvey surfaced anew.

"So 'tis true then, what they say about you and Edward!"

Papa stared at me for long seconds, his blue eyes suddenly hard as ice. When he spoke, his voice was cold and changed: "And what, pray, do they say?"

"That you want to adopt him, and have a proper son to inherit Rosings!" I felt the hot tears spill onto my cheek and began to sob loudly, burying my face in my hands. At first I resisted Papa's attempts to prise them away, so afraid was I of the expression I had glimpsed in those usually mild, kind eyes – but eventually, responding to his entreaties and peeping through my fingers, I saw with relief that he was laughing.

"Anne, Anne, Anne!" he sighed, putting his arms around me and lifting me onto his knee, "Hush your crying, and listen to me. I have no intention of adopting Edward. I have no intention of disinheriting my only child, or any wish to send her away. *You* are the heiress of Rosings, my dear, and you will remain so whomever you shall marry or wherever you shall live. There. I am heartily sorry that your peace of mind has been disturbed by spiteful gossip, and I shall bring Miss Harvey to book for it in no uncertain terms. But I want you to promise me that if ever you are disturbed by such rumour-mongering again, you will come straight to me for the facts of the matter instead of distressing yourself in this way. Will you promise me this, Anne?"

Most gladly did I promise, clinging to Papa as he kissed my brow and wiped away my tears. When finally I slid down from his knee, my equilibrium re-established and my burden eased, I paused before leaving the room to ask shyly, "Papa, will *you* promise not to tell Edward that I said I would like to marry him?"

His blue eyes twinkled as he laid a hand upon his

heart. "Most solemnly. I shall take it to the grave."

I nodded, satisfied, and left him to his library, his thoughts and his letter.

*****chapter five*****

I was not of course privy to the interview that took place between my father and Miss Harvey later that day; an interview that left my governess greatly subdued, but did not result in her dismissal as I had feared it might. Looking back, I can only ascribe Papa's leniency to the knowledge that any harsher course of action would require a full explanation to Mama.

Miss Harvey did not escape unpunished, however: she was given an unsolicited leave of absence to stay with her uncle at Lyme during our upcoming visit to Pemberley – a visit to which I knew she had been greatly looking forward. She put on a good face, declaring herself delighted at the prospect of seeing her guardian again and regaling me with stories of the lively parties to be had at Lyme during the season, and the eligible young men to be met with there.

"I should not be at all surprised, Miss Anne," she said, "If I were to receive a proposal of marriage before the month is out! There are several old beaux of mine whom I shall be sure to encounter. What think you of that? Should I accept, do you think? You would miss me, would you not, if I were to write you as an engaged woman, saying that I would not be returning to Rosings!"

I replied that I would, though I harboured grave doubts as to the likelihood of this eventuality; for if Miss Harvey had such an army of suitors in Lyme, why did she remain unmarried, and a governess? I humoured her however, for in spite of my youth I was sensible of her dependent position and of the resentment it engendered in her. When she left for Lyme, all smiles and adieux, I felt bereft in spite of all the trouble she had caused me.

As my parents prepared for the journey into Derbyshire I quailed inwardly, uncomfortable with the knowledge I now carried regarding my mother's plans for William and myself and fervently wishing that some twist of fate would keep him from home so that I might avoid his company altogether. These worries continued to preoccupy me as the carriage containing Papa, Mama, Mrs Jenkinson and myself swung out of the gates of Rosings and into the lane that led to Hunsford, through which we must pass to gain the open road. Bolstered against the unyielding horsehair by cushions, with a quilt about my knees, I gripped Mrs Jenkinson's hand as we lurched across an uneven scattering of stones and Mama's 'abigail', Dawkins, obliged to travel on the barouche box with the coachman, emitted a series of muffled shrieks. "Poor Dawkins," murmured Papa, as Mama tutted disparagingly.

Mrs Jenkinson and I were seated backward, and I was able to watch the Rectory with its neat box-hedge and garden, the Church with its squat grey Norman tower, and the ramshackle row of cottages which lined the main street of Hunsford recede into the distance as we passed, saluted by a smattering of villagers. As we clattered past the Inn and out onto the open road, I settled myself as best I could for the first stage of our long journey.

By the time we entered the county of Derbyshire two days later I was tired and cross, my eyes heavy from broken sleep in draughty inns and my joints stiff from traveling. I bestirred myself, however, as we drove through the neat little village of Lambton and prepared to enter the Pemberley woods. Magnificent beeches soon formed a canopy over us as we passed the steward's house where old Mr Wickham lived alone with his son following the death of his wife some years ago; I looked back on a tunnel of green and gold as we emerged into sunlight to round the lake, and craned my neck to catch a glimpse of the house with its sweeping lawns and flowerbeds.

The Pemberley estate was no larger than Rosings, but nestling beneath the awe-inspiring sweep of craggy hills it exuded an air of wild grandeur that was quite alien to our gentle Park set amongst the well-mannered gardens of Kent. There was a freedom in the air at Pemberley, a lack of boundaries both within and without doors which I always found unsettling. My little cousin Georgiana tumbled upon her mother's lap, ran about the house as she wished and played in the grounds with the servants' children, much to Mama's disgust. The contrast between her easy playfulness and her brother's haughty formality confused me, leaving me at a loss how to conduct myself so that I often retreated into shyness.

As we entered the familiar drawing-room with its light maple furniture and softly-draped windows, my uncle Darcy came forward to meet us, his bow and greeting genial and welcoming. My aunt held out her arms from the sofa as though to embrace us all, and Georgiana, all rosy cheeks and dark ringlets, slid from her chair and ran towards me crying "Little Anne!" – an epithet by which the Darcys habitually distinguished me from my aunt, but which sounded incongruous on the lips of a child three years my junior.

"Come, my dear, and sit by me. Georgiana, do not push your cousin so!" called my Aunt Darcy from the sofa, as she prepared to receive Mama's embrace and respond to the usual inquiries after her health. She was by this time a partial invalid; three stillbirths had taken their toll upon her strength, chasing the bloom from her cheek and diminishing her womanly figure, though her eyes, dark and luminous, betrayed the lively intelligence that inhabited her fragile body. The arrival of Georgiana, eleven years after William's birth, had done much to restore her spirits; but her demeanor remained gentle and quiet, a striking contrast to Mama's robust, imperious manner.

My aunt was loved by everybody: by her husband, who would personally arrange her cushions and place her footstool; by her children, one of whom now propelled me eagerly towards her sofa while the other stood silent and watchful behind it; by her brother-in-law who bowed affectionately over her proffered hand; and not least by her sister, who embraced her with genuine warmth before seating herself in the chair placed by the footman.

As I approached my aunt's outstretched arms I became aware of William's proximity; he had stepped out from behind the sofa to make his bow, taller than ever, his expression serious beneath a shock of dark curls. A humiliating blush suffused my cheeks.

"Anne? Come come, no shyness! Can you have forgotten us all in so short a time?" laughed my aunt; and Mama, as she busily arranged her skirts, exclaimed, "Oh, she is overwhelmed before so tall and handsome a cousin!"

This was close enough to the truth to cause my blush to deepen further, and Papa, perceiving my confusion and no doubt guessing the cause of it, made a great show of greeting his nephew, ruffling his hair and commenting upon his increased stature in such a way as to draw the general attention away from me.

We usually stayed a month complete with the Darcys, and sensitive though I was to the kindness of my aunt and uncle, I was always ready to leave by the end of it. As the days passed I would begin to find Georgiana's ceaseless chatter irksome, the late hours of the household tiring, the brooding presence of William in the background increasingly uncomfortable; and by the day of our departure I would be looking forward to the predictable routine and undemanding solitude of Rosings. This summer however was to prove entirely different.

Was it because he had emerged from the awkwardness of boyhood, and was well on the way to becoming an adult, that William behaved so differently? Or had my aunt and uncle had taken him to task before our arrival and instructed him to humour his little cousin? However it was, when my aunt suggested that I might like to see the 'fairy bower' built by William for his sister in the woods he calmly acquiesced, took Georgiana's hand with a smile, and politely encouraged me to precede them out into the hallway. While Mrs Jenkinson fussed over my bonnet and Georgiana tugged at my sleeve, I tried in vain to still the painful thudding of my heart at the prospect of being thrust into my future husband's care.

We made our way towards the cool of the woods where smooth grey beeches shone palely against dark green foliage, and Georgiana prattled happily of how 'William and George' - the latter being George Wickham, the steward's son - had brought hazel and willow branches up from the lakeside to fashion her a play house, William began to interject, explaining to me that beechwood was not sufficiently pliant for the task, and that the height and girth of the trunks had forced them to build above a natural hollow in the roots rather than up amongst the branches.

When we reached the place I was certainly impressed; the skillful interweaving of the withies combined with the canopy of leaves high above made the structure almost completely weatherproof, and the interior had been made comfortable with rugs and cushions, upon which several dolls sat propped in readiness for their owner's return. Georgiana fell upon them with cries of delight, and began to set out miniature cups and saucers, inviting me to join her in serving tea whilst William sat back upon his heels and received my compliments upon his handiwork with grave civility.

"Miss Harvey and I made a bower in the small copse at home," I ventured shyly; "We decorated it with almond blossom and read Mr Wordsworth's poetry in it. But we made the roof very ill I think, because when we returned the next day it had fallen in, and we had to ask the gardener to take it away."

William inclined his head politely. "Miss Harvey is your new governess, is she not? She is to your liking, it seems."

"Oh yes!" I responded fervently, and embarked upon a detailed description of my friend and mentor to which he listened patiently until we were interrupted by a shout from outside: "Hullo there! Anybody at home?"

William immediately ducked out from the bower and sprang nimbly up the bank towards the path. "George!" we heard him call, "Come down and join us! My cousin is here - you remember Miss de Bourgh?"

"Oh! Is it George?" cried Georgiana, scrambling out from beneath the branches; and I followed her clumsily, smoothing my dress and dislodging a stray twig from my hair. George Wickham hurried to assist first Georgiana, then myself, up onto the path. He kept possession of my hand as he bowed gracefully, declaring himself honoured to renew my acquaintance and complimenting me upon my increased height. He himself was greatly altered himself since I had last set eyes upon him two years ago; the boyish charm and easy cheerfulness which had always enhanced his blond good looks was now replaced by a confident swagger and a distressingly importunate manner. At sixteen years of age he obviously considered himself something of a ladies' man, and his excessive gallantry discomposed me. I gave a stiff courtesy, unsure how best to respond, and saw William frown and move to step between us. Wickham deferred immediately, releasing my hand and inquiring politely after my journey and my parents' health. As I murmured an answer, Georgiana artlessly seized her friend's hand and declared that he must follow her inside directly and take tea – a demand to which, with a bow in my direction and a wink and a nod to William, he dutifully acquiesced.

"You see how it is," said William, still frowning as we watched them disappear beneath the branches. "My friend Wickham devotes hours to my sister's amusement, and she in turn gives him all the trust of her affectionate nature. My aunt would not approve such familiarity, I think; but his father is an excellent man, and has served our family well. My father has pledged to ensure George's education, and secure him the living at Lambton when he takes the cloth."

"Mr Wickham is to be a clergyman?" I exclaimed; and my cousin's expression and shrug of the shoulders were eloquent as he answered, "Well, that is the plan, though I do not know how he will take to it."

My uncle's liberality towards the Wickhams had already drawn criticism from Mama, who considered the friendship between the Darcy children and a member of the household to be bordering upon impropriety. It was not the sort of thing, she declared, that would be encouraged at Rosings; and indeed I could not imagine that it would, though the childless state of our own taciturn Mr Archer and his equally miserable wife rendered any such discouragement unnecessary. My uncle laughed off her concerns with good humour, pointing out that Wickham was a man of irreproachable character, and that in any event the boy was his godson, whom he was duty bound to encourage. As our visit progressed I began to compare George Wickham's gallantry most unfavourably with William's courteous dignity, and was more than happy to leave him to entertain Georgiana whilst I took walks in the wood with my elder cousin – a circumstance would have further horrified Mama, but which allowed me to delve for the first time beneath the shell of his haughty reticence. To my amazement I discovered him to be not only less disdainful of others than I had assumed, but a young man of thoughtful opinions, fair judgment and good intentions. He did not, for example, share Miss Harvey's salacious interest in the exploits of the Prince of Wales; his sympathies lay entirely with the Princess Caroline, who was, he said, most devoutly to be pitied, being forced to confine herself at Blackheath whilst her husband indulged his extravagance at Brighton.

"I mean no offence to His Highness, of course; but it grieves me to see a man of his stature, who ought to command respect and admiration, set his subjects so poor an example by forsaking his duty in pursuit of pleasure. I would be loath to model my own behaviour upon such a man as he - a drunkard, a gambler, and an unfaithful husband to boot!"

My heart skipped a beat; did he know, I wondered, of our parents' plans for us? Was he letting me know that his behavior as a husband would be irreproachable? Turncoat that I was, I concurred with his every opinion, Miss Harvey all forgotten; and when the day of our departure was announced, I responded for the first time with some dismay.

As we embarked upon the homeward journey with the Darcy farewells ringing in our ears, my father commented, "That was a most enjoyable visit! My nephew was a good deal less constrained with us, I thought, and much more hospitable to Anne. He is coming out of his shell at last."

Mama chose to see this as a latent criticism. "Coming out of his shell, what can you mean?

William has always had perfect manners. You would surely not have him fawn and flatter like the Wickham boy? I have seldom seen so repulsive a display – I wonder my brother-in-law allows it."

This was well-trodden ground, and Papa sighed briefly. "Well well, that is not our business, and the friendship has obviously done young Darcy no harm. I was pleased to see him a little more easy in company, that is all. And as for Georgiana, why, she is blossoming delightfully! Her performance upon the pianoforte was quite remarkable for a child of her age."

Poor Papa – in attempting to turn the conversation he had hit upon a topic that was guaranteed to needle Mama still further My own recital upon the instrument, though it drew polite applause from my aunt and uncle, had been so obviously inferior to my seven year old cousin's that we were neither of us encouraged to play again, the better to spare my blushes. My father's thoughtless remark left me mortified, while Mama declared angrily that her niece's constant prattle gave her the headache, and that she had advised her sister to lose no time in hiring a governess to instill some discipline into the child.

Papa shrugged helplessly. "Well, at least Anne has enjoyed her visit, and taken pleasure in her cousins' society – is it not so, Anne?"

My acquiescence restored the peace; Mama nodded with satisfaction, repeating some compliment that my uncle had paid me and praising my tolerance of Georgiana. She then turned the conversation to my Aunt Darcy's health, her poor appetite and the fatigue which prevented her from taking beneficial exercise. It was a topic of genuine concern to her, and as Papa sought to allay her fears for her sister I nestled into Mrs Jenkinson's shoulder once more and allowed my thoughts to drift, my memory lingering upon William's smile, the pleasure of his conversation and his parting promise, the first of its kind, to write to me.

That visit to Pemberley is etched upon my memory as the last time I ever saw my poor Aunt Darcy. Early in the following year she succumbed to a chill which she was unable to shake off, and she died just a few days into Lent.

We went back up for the funeral. The occasion was made all the more terrible for me by the contrast with our happy visit just nine months previously; by the starkness of the bare beeches, skeletal against a bleached sky; by the ashen face of my poor uncle; by Georgiana's tears, and by William's silence. He was unreachable in his grief, replying to my timid condolences only with a bow. Georgiana, white as a paper doll in her stiff black dress, sat quietly upon the high pew, never once letting go her father's hand. When the funeral supper was over we left immediately, making the first leg of our journey in the dying light of a February afternoon.

Mama's grief for her sister was restrained, but genuine. Several times I observed her raise a handkerchief discreetly to her eyes during the funeral oration, and she was uncharacteristically quiet throughout our stay. It was not until we passed the steward's lodge and turned out onto the road for the journey home that she commented, "At least Anne was happy in her marriage; she was fortunate in *that* respect. He adored her, you know; my brother-in-law adored her, as a wife *should* be adored. I always envied her that."

Papa was wise enough not to respond, and the first leg of our journey was accomplished in silence. I was was left to endure the bumpy ride as best I could, and to wonder for the first time what difference it might have made to my mother if she had been adored, as a wife *should* be adored.

*****chapter six*****

Time passed. Edward became a Captain, and was placed in charge of a Company. He continued to visit us whenever he had leave from his regiment, which was a pleasure both to Papa and to me. William went up to Cambridge, and we did not see him for some time: Mama could not bear to visit Pemberley during the year of her sister's death, and when we did eventually make the journey he was from home. I was shocked to see how tired and aged my poor uncle now appeared, though he received us kindly, assuring us of William's best wishes and speaking proudly of his progress and good conduct. George Wickham was now also at Cambridge, and to Georgiana, bereft of companionship, I was obviously a welcome guest. Once the initial reserve consequent upon two years' separation had worn off, we continued more or less where we had left off – that is, she lavished sisterly affection upon me, and I found her both as charming and as irritating as a little sister can be. She did not appear to be haunted by grief as I had feared she might be; she possessed, I now realise, the natural resilience of a child in the face of bereavement and change.

Then came the announcement of the Honourable Mr John Fitzwilliam's engagement to a Miss Augusta Morton, only daughter of an English baronet and a sufficiently desirable match to tempt him, in his thirtieth year, from the profligate bachelorhood that was fast becoming the despair of his father and aunt. Their summer wedding brought our three families – the Fitzwilliams, the de Bourghs and the Darcys – together at Evesham House in Hampshire, ancestral seat of the Earls of Amberleigh. It was a place I had visited but seldom, and I felt all the timidity of a stranger upon entering the lofty hallway with its black and white tiled floor and preponderance of marble busts. I was pleased to see Edward, looking very grand in his regimentals but still the same familiar friend, waiting there to meet us. His company did much to alleviate my shyness before the arrival of the Darcys on the following day.

William, just down from Cambridge, now exuded a confidence and maturity that left me initially tongue-tied. He greeted me kindly, however, commenting that I looked exceedingly well; there was something in his eyes as he said it that told me he was equally taken aback by the changes wrought in the space of three years.

"Do you not think our cousin Anne has grown, Darcy?" teased Edward when he joined us in the morning room; "She is almost fourteen now – quite a lady, and quite the most important of all the bridesmaids. She has brought her own personal entourage with her – not only good Mrs Jenkinson but also the interesting Miss Harvey, whose personal history grows ever more intriguing. It seems that her father, whom I could have sworn was a Naval man, was actually a Sergeant of Artillery, though she cannot name either his battalion or his Captain. I wonder she has never mentioned it before. I did not like to intrude upon her conversation with my brother's friend, however, in search of clarification; I was overlistening, you see. A deplorable habit."

I blushed, embarrassed once more by my governess' lack of subtlety and unrivaled capacity for invention. "I have only ever heard that Miss Harvey's father was a Lieutenant of Marines," I murmured, and Edward laughed.

"Well, he must have been a prodigiously active fellow to have served both in the Marines and the Artillery. A veritable chameleon. And his daughter takes after him, I suspect. What is your opinion, Anne?"

"Miss Harvey tells many different stories," I admitted reluctantly. Edward laughed again, and patted my shoulder, but William's dark brows met in a frown.

"Miss Harvey is very free with her conversation, it seems. She had better not try to draw *me.*"

"She would not be so bold," smiled Edward. "Everyone knows, Darcy, that it requires considerable persistence and ingenuity to engage *you* in conversation even amongst equals!"

"That is a censure I do not deserve, cousin! We cannot all perform to strangers. You are blessed with a sociable disposition and a pleasing manner, and your goodwill is generously bestowed; I am put to greater effort to be pleasant in company, and prefer to reserve my good opinion for those deserving of it."

He bowed towards me slightly as he spoke, to indicate that I was included amongst the deserving few, and I blushed and smiled my thanks. I would have liked to continue the conversation, but Georgiana tugged urgently at my hand announcing that the bridal party were just arrived and that if we hurried to the window we could watch the ladies being handed down.

My cousin John had a modern man's impatience with convention, and on this occasion had persuaded my uncle to break with it on two counts, much to Mama's disgust. Miss Morton's father, a gentleman of romantic persuasion, spent the greater part of the year in Brighton or Bath where his daughter and young second wife could enjoy fashionable company while his Devonshire estate was let to a retired naval officer. It had therefore been decided that the wedding would take place from Evesham, and my uncle had offered to accommodate the bride and her family in the East Wing for two nights, that they might rest from the rigours of their journey and make themselves at ease. In addition, my cousin had purchased a special license to save his guests the trouble of rising early; the ceremony, in the little parish church where my parents themselves had married sixteen years earlier, was to take place at one in the afternoon. Mama found both arrangements highly indecorous, but there was nothing she could do; her brother had approved them, and as we were guests under his roof she could not give vent to her opinions openly.

The arrival of the bridal party did nothing to mitigate her disapproval. There was a large contingent of fashionable young people amongst them, relatives for the most part of the bride's stepmother. Their unrestrained manners and lively conversation were a source of fascination to Georgiana and myself, while the dandyish attire of the gentlemen drew comment from Papa, who marveled that with clothes so tight and necks so swathed they could move without injury. Edward, to whom the remark was chiefly addressed, suggested they take lessons from Mr Brummel, "who is now the oracle of all matters sartorial in London and Brighton, and has decreed that if a gentleman dresses in such a way as to make people turn to stare, he is not well dressed."

I did not suppose Miss Augusta Morton would much care for such advice; even allowing for a bride's prerogative to be first in company, be the others who they may, her determination to take centre stage was somewhat extreme. Her conversation was punctuated with so many little screams, Italian phrases and fluttering of the hands as to cause me to forget my manners and stare at her openly, while Papa's declaration that he had never seen so many bows and tassels upon one gown received a hearty endorsement from Mama whose sense of decorum was hourly outraged by the vulgarity paraded before her.

I repeated some of her disparaging remarks to Miss Harvey, in hopes of her drawing some comfort from them. Insubstantial as any expectations regarding the Honourable Mr John Fitzwilliam must always have been for her, it could not but pain my governess to go completely unacknowledged by him in his own house. She accepted her invisible place in the proceedings with as good a grace as she could muster, but I did feel sorry for her and was surprised when, contrary as always, she championed her erstwhile suitor's bride.

"What do you know of fashionable society, Miss Anne?" she scoffed; "For all you are heiress of Rosings Park, you are quite the country bumpkin. Why, Mrs Fitzwilliam, as she will be tomorrow, will be quite the latest thing, admired by the whole of London society; by the time you are old enough to be presented at Court she will very likely be Countess of Amberleigh and considered a model for young women to aspire to, whatever your Mama may say. I'd advise you to sit up and start to take notice; when I was your age I knew a good deal more of the world, I can tell you!"

I was stung by this, and my retort, "I'm sure I need not take lessons from you, Miss Harvey, in how to behave as a lady!" discomposed her momentarily; but she rallied herself to comment that I obviously supposed myself very grand today, "Just like your cousin, the grand Mr Darcy, who thinks himself above the conversation of perfectly respectable people. A tedious husband *he* will make, I shouldn't be surprised. A fine dull marriage you two will have, and no mistake!"

I left her alone after that; I knew there was no pleasing Miss Harvey when she was disposed to be otherwise. I surmised that William had snubbed her, and the thought upset me enough to seek proof that he was not really too proud to be friendly towards his inferiors. When I next had opportunity to converse with him I inquired after George Wickham, asking whether he saw much of his friend at Cambridge. His response was not encouraging.

"I saw him as little as possible, Anne, and what I did see distressed me exceedingly. Heaven knows what liberties he will allow himself in his final year, without my presence to curb him. He is not turning out at all as we hoped; I have said nothing about it at home, but if his behaviour continues along present lines he will end a great disappointment to my father and to his own."

I pressed eagerly for more information, but William frowned and shook his head. "I will not distress you with the details Anne, especially as you are still little more than a child; but you must believe me when I tell you he is not fit company for any respectable lady. My father intends him for the Church as you know, but a man less suited to the cloth I have yet to encounter. If he continues as he is now, I will no longer be able to admit his company."

"I am very sorry to hear it," I faltered, amazed. "You seemed such good friends when I saw you together last, at Pemberley."

"Friendships alter," said William grimly, "as characters unfold."

I was silent, remembering my own uneasy impression of George Wickham; his excessive gallantry, his fawning flattery, his consciousness of his own good looks. *'Friendships alter as characters unfold'* - it was a sobering thought.

The wedding day passed off magnificently, and I could not help but enjoy myself. In the morning I was pinched and preened into a stiff white taffeta gown, with Mrs Jenkinson adorning my sash with rosebuds and Miss Harvey lamenting the absence of an extra row of frilled lace at my neck. I was plainly attired however in comparison with the other bridesmaids - Miss Morton's younger cousins - and was relieved when Georgiana, who was to share with me the task of scattering rose petals in the bride's path, appeared in a simple muslin gown and bonnet adorned only with blue ribbon.

We carried out our duties with tolerable grace, I think; my abiding memory of our progress down the aisle is of the bride's cream silk slippers and the hem of her gown, heavily embroidered with silver thread and pearls. The ceremony itself seemed interminable, and I spent most of it studying the gold brocade on the groom's green waistcoat, which snaked and looped as his substantial stomach rose and fell.

The sumptuousness of the wedding breakfast, during which I drank rather more white soup and sweet chocolate than was good for me, left me feeling slightly unwell; when the dancing began I was forbidden by Mama to leave my chair.

As Georgiana and I watched the couples advance and retreat across the floor, with a restless Miss Harvey seated between us as chaperone, I looked eagerly for William and Edward amongst the dancers. I soon spotted Edward gallantly escorting an talkative lady onto the floor, but William I could not see anywhere. Then the line of couples parted momentarily before me and I caught a glimpse of him across the room, standing quiet and solemn before one of the great windows, watching the proceedings attentively. How handsome he is, I mused: eyes luminous in a face of chiseled ivory, jaw clean and manly, nose perfectly straight, hair dark and abundant like his sister's. His mouth appeared perhaps a little small, but it was his habit to keep his lips pressed tightly together. He did not smile for all and sundry: *'we cannot all perform to strangers'.* That was why he did not dance, though several ladies were seated about the room fanning themselves vigorously at the approach of every gentleman. As I continued to study him unobserved, he shifted his gaze and saw me. He did not return my smile but made a graceful bow in my direction, keeping his eyes upon my face until the swirl of dancers surged between us, obliterating him from view. I felt a flush suffuse my cheeks; my heart was racing and a tingling rose upwards from my knees, a disturbing sensation which I was half inclined to blame upon the white soup, though I suspected it had little to do with the intricacies of digestion. When I next looked for him across the room, he had gone.

The bride and groom were to spend their first months as man and wife at my uncle's house in town, the better to enjoy their privacy whilst also having ample opportunity to show themselves off in public. By the time their carriage departed amidst a shower of good wishes I was dizzy with excitement and fatigue, and Mama insisted I retire to bed early along with Georgiana. I was in no state to resist and drifted off to sleep quickly enough, surfacing to consciousness late in the evening to see the sky outside the window just turning to indigo, and Miss Harvey crying quietly in the alcove seat where she sat mending a tear in my taffeta gown. I watched her with drowsy compassion until sleep dragged me back under, to dream of cream silk slippers, dancing couples, and the dark, steady gaze of a young man's eyes.

*****chapter seven*****

The orderly routine of Rosings seemed very dull after the excitement of the wedding. The hay harvest was in full progress when we returned, and Mama immediately immersed herself once more in the affairs of Hunsford, leaving Papa to observe my restless demeanour and inquire whether first taste of society had left me hungry for more.

"We lead an unfashionably sedate life here, Anne," he said, "and a young girl like yourself, fast growing towards womanhood, is bound to feel the restriction of it. But do not despair; there are balls and assemblies enough in Kent, and in another couple of years you shall have have your fill of them. I may even attend myself, for the pleasure of seeing you dance! Which leads me to make a suggestion: what say you, in the meantime, to dancing lessons from a professional master?"

I assented eagerly, and Mama, when applied to, decided to go further; she proposed that we take a house in London for six weeks from the mid-September, that I might have the benefit of increased society and study drawing, dancing and music with reputable masters. It would give me some much-needed confidence, she declared, in preparation for my presentation at Court in three years' time, and if the experiment proved successful we might make it an annual arrangement.

Miss Harvey, to her chagrin, did not accompany us to town, and under Mrs Jenkinson's more sober custody I encountered none of the gossip and scandal that my governess would have deemed an essential ingredient of life in the metropolis. Our society was confined to a few suitable families, friends of my mother, whose daughters like myself were sedate and unadventurous. Nevertheless I enjoyed myself greatly and as Mama predicted I gained confidence from my lessons, learning to negotiate my way around the dance floor with tolerable skill and producing a few pleasing sketches and watercolours. The music master, unwilling to lose a valuable patronage, provided me with some deceptively easy pieces which I could perform without stumbling by the end of the month, and Mama was delighted with the success of her scheme. To my delight she engaged a young man from Rochester to continue my dancing lessons upon our return to Rosings; and Miss Harvey, while pronouncing Mr Langham to be 'a milksop and a nincompoop', soon looked forward to his visits as much as I for the opportunity it gave her to indulge her penchant for London gossip with a fellow enthusiast.

In December, my parents arranged a private party at Rosings to which my cousins, together with a few carefully chosen families of the neighbourhood, were invited. This gave me opportunity to try out my skills upon the dance floor in an informal setting. Not even the contrast between my mediocre effort at the pianoforte and Georgiana's bravura performance could sour my felicity. Mama was loud in her praise of me, but it was William's quiet compliment upon my lightness of foot which caused me to tingle with pleasure. His own dancing was, I had to admit, inferior to Edward's, but the grave concentration with which he handed me about the floor, and the appreciation in his dark gaze, more than compensated for any woodenness of movement. The Fitzwilliams had excused themselves on account of the delicate condition of 'Cousin Augusta', the outcome of which was expected late in Spring. I was glad of it for Miss Harvey's sake, and pleased to observe that Edward and two or three other gentlemen had the thoughtfulness to ask her to dance.

With hindsight I would recollect how tired and ill my uncle Darcy looked during that visit, how slowly he moved, how heavily he leaned upon the bannister when ascending the staircase; but at the time, riding high on a wave of newly acquired confidence, I was too self-absorbed to think it worthy of note. He was as kind towards me as ever, still calling me 'little Anne' in deference to his beloved wife. I was soon to wish I had shown him more reciprocal affection.

We were gathered in the drawing room some three months later when the message arrived. It was late afternoon, and the light was fading; Mrs Jenkinson was just advising me to set down my embroidery lest I succumbed to eyestrain when the sound of an arrival on horseback and a commotion of voices in the hallway prepared us for a matter of urgency. We all turned toward the door, and my father rose as Wilson entered bearing an envelope upon the tray.

"An express has arrived for you, Sir."

Mama's loud inquiries remained unanswered while he read it; but then he placed the letter in her hands, saying quietly "I am so sorry, my dear. It happened at Pemberly yesterday morning."

"It is Mr Darcy," he explained, turning to Mrs Jenkinson and myself; "I am afraid he was taken ill quite suddenly; they think it was his heart. I am heartily grieved for my poor niece and nephew."

While Mrs Jenkinson rummaged for Mama's smelling salts and sent for Dawson to attend her, Papa embraced me briefly, holding my face in his hands as the tears welled up. "Be brave, Anne," he admonished; "Your uncle is gone where he has long wished to be; he is reunited with his dear wife. We must do all we can for your cousins."

The funeral of Mr George Darcy was as grand an affair as his greatness and popularity deserved. In addition to the household, the entire village of Lambton seemed to be gathered at the Church gates; many people were openly sobbing. It occurred to me that my uncle must have been a good man indeed to be loved by so many. The funeral oration praised his generosity as a landlord, his tireless concern for his household and tenants; as I listened I understood for the first time how great a responsibility came with the inheritance of an estate. My mind wandering selfishly as the minds of young people do, I wondered whether the good people of Hunsford held my father in similar regard. I knew that Mama was respected, but not loved; when accompanying her on parish errands I was frequently mortified by the manner in which she brushed aside the concerns and opinions of her inferiors. Even amongst equals, her lack of sensitivity and forthright opinions often gave unwitting offence. Though my natural reticence would surely preserve me from similar error, I had received little instruction in the skills needed to earn the affection of one's household, neighbours and tenants as my Aunt and Uncle Darcy had done.

At the funeral supper William was distant towards me, retreating into his shell as he had done when his mother died. It fell to me to provide company and comfort for poor Georgiana who poured out her grief without restraint, bewailing the loss of so affectionate a father and renewing her sorrow for her mother with all the passion of her young heart. I consoled her as best I could, assuring her that my parents would join with William in caring for her, and promising always to be her friend and confidante. George Wickham was present with his elderly father, but having saluted us respectfully he kept his distance; his grief for his godfather seemed genuine, and I hoped it would go some way towards healing the rift between himself and William.

It transpired that my father was not, after all, to join William in the guardianship of Georgiana. That honour had been bequeathed by her parents to Edward, much to everyone's surprise. Mama felt the slight keenly on my father's behalf, but was obliged to keep her objections to herself whilst Edward remained in our company; and as he joined us for the journey home as far as London she was uncharacteristically silent in the carriage, giving me ample time to ponder something that was just beginning to impinge upon me: at the age of just two and twenty, my future husband was now the master of Pemberley.

Back at Rosings, my mother gave vent to her feelings. "To give a young girl into the care of Edward Fizwilliam! What was my poor brother Darcy thinking? Ridiculous. 'Tis an insult to you, my dear, and to my brother likewise!"

"It is nothing of the kind," was Papa's measured response; "Darcy could not count on either myself or your brother outliving him, and knew that John was likely to be burdened with family responsibilities of his own. Edward is an excellent choice. He is in every way qualified to look after his cousin's affairs, and her brother will value his advice. If anything, God forbid, should happen to William before my niece comes of age, she will have a wise and loving protector in her cousin."

"Protector!" snorted Mama; "what does he know of the responsibilities of looking after a young girl? He shows no inclination to marry, of course – now *that* should have been a condition of guardianship – and besides, he will soon be away fighting the

French, and may very likely be killed in action, and die sooner than any of us!"

I paused in the task of knotting my embroidery, my needle poised in mid-air as Papa composed himself before replying, with forced calm, "You seem to have forgotten, my dear, that our brother Darcy planned to send Georgiana to school in London when she reached a suitable age; an excellent idea that I hope her guardians will adhere to. She will be able to enjoy the society of her own sex, and benefit from the guidance into womanhood that a motherless child might otherwise lack. I really think we need have no fears for her future."

School! I gasped audibly, though Mama ignored me, stabbing angrily at the air with her finger: "That exactly proves my point! Captain Fitzwilliam places his ward in a school where she will be exposed to who knows what unsuitable influences, and disappears off with his Regiment, likely never to return. How is *that* responsible guardianship?"

"Come now, my dear," sighed Papa wearily, "There are many excellent establishments where a young lady may complete her education quite safely without being exposed to undesirable influences."

"I wish I could share your complacency! It is not a risk I would consider taking with Anne. If my brother had seen fit to consult *me* upon the subject, I would have advised most strenuously against it."

"I am sure you would, Catherine. I am sure you would." Here my father rose from his seat and exited the room, putting an end to further debate.

This was but one of many similar conversations overheard by me, but the first in which I learned of my cousin's impending good fortune. Miss Harvey had often regaled me with stories of her schooldays: tales of secret assignations, love letters hidden in gloves, mistresses bribed to turn a blind eye, scandals, elopements and suchlike. If even half were to be believed, my mother's concerns regarding school education were perfectly justified! My own imaginings were more modest; shy though I was, I was beginning to feel the lack of friends of my own age and sex keenly, and to dream of being able to share secrets, confidences and gossip with other girls. And now this happy lot would fall to Georgiana, whilst I remained solitary at Rosings!

"Just imagine," crowed Miss Harvey upon hearing the news, "What beaux your cousin will attract in London! She will be greatly admired for her family alone, and with looks and accomplishments such as hers she is sure to be the centre of attention. What gossip she will be able to write of! And *you* will be her chief correspondent, for she is not likely to tell her brother the half of it. You will have to learn to keep secrets from your future husband, Miss Anne!"

In the days that followed I reminded myself repeatedly that my cousin was an orphan, bereft of both parents, and greatly to be pitied; but it did no good. The shameful truth was that I was cruelly and selfishly jealous.

*****chapter eight*****

Autumn came round once more, and again my parents took a house in London. William and Georgiana were also in town, visiting and assessing schools. They returned Papa's call promptly – a wise move, since it greatly mollified Mama and secured her belated approval of the whole scheme. She inquired meticulously into the sizes and situations of the establishments under consideration, and was only narrowly dissuaded from visiting them all herself the better to assess their suitability; I derived some amusement from observing how skilfully William gave the appearance of deferring to my mother whilst continuing to act solely upon his own judgment. She approved his final choice - a small ladies' establishment in Grosvenor Square – on the grounds of its proximity to the Earl of Durham's residence.

When Georgiana and I spoke alone, she reacted to my protestations of envy with astonishment. She could not imagine why anyone would think her fortunate to be sent away from home; she had been perfectly happy with her governess, and would miss the familiar household of Pemberly sorely. Most of all, she would miss her brother, whose visits would be her only consolation; though she confided to me shyly that someone else had promised to call upon her – George Wickham, who was resident in London studying the law.

I was amazed to hear this. "Is he not then to be a clergyman? I thought my uncle had granted him a living!"

Georgiana shook her head. "No, that is all changed. When his father died, he wrote a letter to William -"

"Old Mr Wickham is dead? When did this happen? Who is managing the estate?"

"Oh, it happened not long after – after Papa." Here she paused to swallow and I held out my hands to her, sorry to have touched upon so tender a subject. She took them gratefully, moved closer to me upon the sofa, and continued unsteadily: "Mr Wickham was so very fond of Papa, you see. Mr Rowe is our steward now – I do not like him half so well. But George – that is, young Mr Wickham – has decided to study the law instead of taking holy orders, and it has made William angry. He will not call on him, though he knows where he is lodging. And he does not know that George has written to me, because he was from home when the letter arrived – you will not tell him, will you Anne? George writes that 'tis all a misunderstanding, and we shall very soon all be friends again, and my brother will not mind him visiting me. I shall feel so much better knowing he is nearby."

I was cruelly torn, but after some deliberation I decided to respect my cousin's confidence and say nothing of this to William. He did not mention George Wickham, even when recounting to Mama the story of his father's sudden death and the appointment of Mr Rowe; and I, basking in his approval of my kindness to Georgiana, did not wish to run the risk of arousing his displeasure.

On the day before my cousins returned to Pemberley we all walked together in St James' Park, strolling leisurely beneath the trees with the rest of fashionable London. It was a beautiful September day, indolent and golden, the boughs above us heavy with late summer leaves that filtered the afternoon sunlight. My mother encountered an old acquaintance and stopped for the obligatory exchange of pleasantries, detaining Georgiana whilst William and I walked on unawares. When we turned to look for them Mama waved and nodded, pointing me out to the bewigged dowager who raised a lorgnette to survey us. I blushed, imagining the import of her conversation, and blushed again to think that Georgiana must overhear it. When I turned back to William he was observing me closely, which only increased my mortification. Without a word he offered me his arm, and I allowed him to escort me to a convenient bench where we could sit until they joined us. I was acutely conscious of the picture that we must present, so pleasing to Mama and so eloquent to her friend, whilst at the same time experiencing the perturbation of Willliam's close proximity. I sighed unconsciously as we seated ourselves, and he asked whether I were fatigued.

It was a simple enough inquiry, but the breath caught in my throat as I met those dark eyes. Quickly lowering my gaze I murmured a negative. A breeze sighed in the trees above us and he adjusted my shawl, saying, "I would not have you lose that delicate bloom, Anne; you must take care of yourself for me."

It was an occasion of no note to anyone passing by, and when Mama and Georgiana joined us they seemed insensible of the change in the air that almost caused my knees to buckle as I rose, supported by William's strong arm; but I knew that an understanding had just passed between us. For the first time, he had asserted the right to care for me as something more than a cousin; for the first time, I had openly and publicly accepted his protection. At the age of just fifteen I imagined myself to have found love, and to have found it easily, without having to undergo the tests of endurance and fidelity that Miss Burney's novels deemed a necessary part of the process. Looking back, I can only wonder at my own credulity.

In such a heady state, I scarcely noticed Miss Harvey's air of secrecy and self-importance upon our return to Rosings, or wondered at her request for a private interview with my parents. I knew she had visited Lyme during our absence, and was ready to be entertained by her usual anecdotes of naval officers and parties; but I was completely unprepared for the momentous announcement I received in the schoolroom on the following day.

My governess was engaged to be married! She would be leaving Rosings in a matter of weeks. My initial astonishment gave way to excitement, proposals and husbands being much on my mind, and I was as eager to hear as she was to relate all the details of so sudden a transformation of her prospects.

The gentleman in question was a Mr Younge, a solicitor from London who had been holidaying in Lyme; they had met over cards at an evening hosted by Captain Fairchild. Mr Younge's income, though never clearly stated, was obviously sufficient for Miss Harvey to look favourably upon the offer of marriage he made her after a mere fortnight's acquaintance; she described him as a 'mature gentleman, with exquisite manners' and assured me that his proposal was 'most elegantly phrased'.

"He said, *'Miss Harvey, in the short time I have known you your beauty has sent Cupid's arrow winging its way to my heart, and I must speak: will you do me the very great honour of consenting to become my wife?'* And he was holding my hand all the while, with tears in his eyes! Only think Miss Anne – I shall be married by Christmas, and living in town to boot! Lord knows I have waited long enough, and all on your account too – I could have been married several times over were it not for my attachment to you and to Rosings, but I vowed never to abandon my charge and I flatter myself I have kept my word. You are fifteen now, and will do well enough without me."

I was rather sceptical as to the truth of all this self-denial, for as far as I knew this was the first proposal

Miss Harvey had ever received, but I was wise enough not to challenge her on the matter. I had long been aware of her discontent with her situation; her position at Rosings had not brought her the opportunities she had been hoping for, and I could not blame her for jumping at the chance to quit it. I expressed admiration for Mr Younge's mode of expression, which I secretly thought somewhat pompous, wished her joy and hoped that she would bring her husband to visit us after the wedding.

My parents were surprised but not displeased by Miss Harvey's announcement; she would have finished her duties as my governess within a year or two in any case, and my mother at least believed her to have discharged them satisfactorily. Much as she boasted of the pains taken over my education, Mama had paid only sporadic visits to the schoolroom and was blissfully unaware of the glaring gaps in my knowledge of the weightier subjects. Papa of course had no such illusions; but as long as I shared his enjoyment of literature, spoke French pleasingly and had a working knowledge of the Classics he was content to let things be. Neither had any idea how frequently Miss Harvey had mocked and abused them behind their backs. Having satisfied herself that my governess was not marrying above her station, Mama joined my father in wishing her joy.

As for me, I would miss my confidante sorely, though my opinion of her had matured somewhat over our six years' acquaintance and I could not but feel some relief at being spared the task of hiding my feelings for William from her mocking scrutiny. When Georgiana's first letter from Grosvenor Square arrived, full of enthusiasm for her new life, lively friends and comfortable environment, at least I had news to convey by return!

Mr and Mrs Younge did visit in the new year, and I was horrified to discover this 'mature gentleman with exquisite manners' to be portly and middle aged, much given to noisily clearing his throat and dabbing a handkerchief to his glistening brow. He was certainly disposed to make himself agreeable, and paid me a great many compliments to which I scarcely knew how to respond, so taken aback was I by his failure to meet my expectations. No wonder he had been so easily smitten by Miss Harvey's charms – he must hardly have been able to believe his luck! I'm sure he found me very proud and distant, for I said as little to him as possible; but he pleased Mama by making a long speech of thanks for the comfortable home and superior company which his bride had enjoyed whilst residing with us, and Mrs Younge, as I must now call her, appeared happy enough, making a great show of the ring upon her finger and bidding me a gleefully affectionate farewell.

With my governess well and truly gone, I was thrown back upon the gentle company of Mrs Jenkinson, to whom I expressed my dismay over Mr Younge in no uncertain terms. She was amused by my vehemence, and shook her head with a knowing smile.

"Come come, my dear, what did you expect? Miss Harvey knew full well that she could not afford to be particular in the matter of suitors. She was not going to refuse him simply because he does not meet the romantic expectations of a young girl; she had weightier matters to consider. As Mr Younge's wife she will be settled, independent and respectable, and she has resources of character enough to make friends and occupy herself pleasantly in London. I can see your disappointment, my chicken, but there is really no need to feel sorry for her; Mrs Younge has as fair a chance of happiness as most can boast on entering the marriage state."

I supposed, reluctantly, that she must be right; but I fervently thanked Heaven that my own future husband was much better suited to a young girl's romantic expectations, and that I would never be brought to such a pass as to have to consider an alliance with the likes of Mr Younge!

****chapter nine*****

Following Miss Harvey's departure, Mama engaged various masters to continue my instruction. The music master was quickly dismissed, having been unwise enough to inform her that I possessed little aptitude for the instrument and that my singing voice was weak. My French was praised, however, as was my drawing, and I continued to read literature, history and the classics from Papa's library. My dancing lessons continued and I took pride in my light, buoyant step and neat footwork, and began to dream of the coming-out ball that was to sweeten my dreaded presentation at Court when I turned seventeen. I rode out on horseback daily, and my health and spirits blossomed. Much as I missed my governess, I enjoyed the independence that her departure bequeathed me. Stepping out from the shadow of her influence, I found myself able to enjoy my life and all its privileges without shame or fear of ridicule.

It concerned me that Mama had still said not one word to me about marriage. She made many allusions to Pemberley and often invited me to join her in praising William, particularly in company, but she never referred outright to the expectation of his one day being her son-in-law. I found myself becoming impatient with so uncharacteristic a reticence; what could she mean by it? Did she judge me too young, at nearly sixteen, to be included in plans for my own future? I knew her to disapprove of early marriage – she had often remarked that a bride of fifteen was little more than a child, and voiced her approval of the strictures placed upon the Prince of Wales forbidding him from marrying before the age of five and twenty. William would be five and twenty in eighteen months' time; was that what Mama was waiting for? Or was the matter not to be spoken of before my coming-out, in which case she must imagine that Queen Charlotte's touch would miraculously equip me with all the requisite qualities for married life. I began to take matters into my own hands, aware of the responsibility that could soon be placed upon my narrow shoulders; my newfound interest in dinner menus, kitchen garden management and the contents of linen cupboards was encouraged by Mrs Henderson, but completely ignored by Mama. Did she not realise, I wondered indignantly, that I had much to learn before I could take my place as mistress of Pemberley? Yet I lacked the courage to broach the subject.

When I returned one fine May morning from a bracing ride around the Park to be informed that Papa wished to see me in the library, I paused only to unbutton my redingote and shake the cherry blossom from my hair before taking the stairs at a somewhat unladylike pace; so convinced was I that William and Pemberley must be the subjects of our conversation that my heart was thumping in my chest as I knocked and entered.

Papa looked up from his book with a welcoming smile. "Well Anne, you look remarkably pretty today! Riding agrees with you, I see, and the spring air has put a glow to your cheeks. Be seated, my dear; I have some news that I think will please you. I have been speaking with your mother, and have finally persuaded her to allow you to complete your education with a year at a ladies' seminary in London. And not just any ladies' seminary – the Misses Smithson's establishment in Grosvenor Square, where your cousin Georgiana is currently enjoying herself so much. It is all arranged, subject only to your approval and consent; we will go up in September as usual, and return home without you! What say you to that?"

Once I had recovered from my astonishment, I had a great many appreciative things to say, as well as questions to ask. In the days and weeks following I also experienced a multitude of qualms, for when dreams come true we find ourselves less prepared for their manifestation in actuality than we had been in fantasy. Correspondence between myself and Georgiana flew thick and fast: I spent hours curled up in the window seat of the old schoolroom, scribbling questions and confiding scruples, all thoughts of maturity and responsibility temporarily shelved. My cousin had now been at school for the best part of a year, and had much to advise regarding the fashion for long-sleeves, the rashness of imparting confidences on first acquaintance, and the necessity of knowing which schoolmistresses would endorse the smuggling in of comestibles. She promised to be my guide in all things, and hoped that my residence at the seminary might soften her brother's opposition to her receiving visits from George Wickham, a matter on which he had been hitherto inflexible. And of course she would be at Pemberley for the summer, and looked forward to our annual visit when we could converse, confide and make plans face to face.

How happily I was anticipating that visit! Not only was I eager to see Georgiana, but of course *he* would be there, and the prospect of renewing the understanding that had passed between us ten months previously set my nerves a-tingle. Such a heady mixture of eagerness and trepidation was impossible to hide from Papa's observant gaze. He cautioned me more than once to keep a level head, assuring me that if I found myself unequal to the challenge of school life I had but to write and he would come and take me home. The memory of his fatherly tenderness during those weeks is still hard to bear; riding high on a wave of excitement and anticipation, I paid scant heed to the wistful expression in his eyes when he said he would miss me. But such is the nature of Time, most inexorable of life's conditions; we live every moment in foolish anticipation of the next, heedless of the tide that can surge without warning to change the landscape of our future, carrying all our hopes and plans away in its ebb.

Well, I have put off the telling of it for long enough, and now write it I must. On a beautiful July morning in the year 1807 my father was thrown from his horse whilst riding to Hunsford, and sustained a fatal blow to the head. We never discovered what had startled the horse – it was not his usual mount, trusty old Charlemagne, but a younger, skittish gelding he had recently acquired, which may have reared at a fox or a rabbit darting across the lane.

I was sitting with Mama in the morning room, re-reading one of Georgiana's letters while she discussed the dinner menu with Mrs Henderson, when the door was flung open without ceremony and a flurry of servants demanded our attention. One of the gardeners was hauled breathless before us, stammering that he had seen his master leave the Park on horseback at a fine gallop, heard a whinny and a shout of alarm from beyond the hedge not one minute later, and had run out to find the horse standing motionless beside Sir Lewis' prone body. Jarvis and Wilson were bringing him indoors, and one of the grooms had been dispatched for the doctor.

Mama immediately quitted the room, calling out as she did so for Mrs Jenkinson to attend me; she did not allow me to go downstairs when Papa was brought into the hall upon a stretcher. It was not until he had been carried up to his room and laid carefully upon the bed, attended by Dr Harris and drugged with possets, that I was allowed to see him.

His face upon the pillow was as white as the bandage that swathed it; his eyes were closed and his breathing rapid and shallow.

Mrs Jenkinson kept her arm around me, speaking in low, calm tones, trying to reassure me that all might yet be well; but I knew from Dr Harris' serious manner, from the tiptoeing of the servants as they entered and left the room with shocked faces, from the way Mama sat with head bowed and hands clasped so tightly that the knuckles showed white, that Death had come to Rosings and stood waiting at the bed's foot, and that this, incredibly, was the last goodbye.

As the long afternoon progressed, Mrs Henderson persuaded Mama to go below and take some refreshment. I immediately took her place at the bedside, while Mrs Jenkinson sat quietly by the door.

The curtains had been partly drawn and we sat in artificial twilight, I constantly imagining some change in those still features, some movement of the lips or flicker of the eyelids. I whispered words of love and comfort, wiping the tears that coursed my cheeks with one hand whilst I held his cold fingers in the other. How slim and white those fingers were, how beautifully shaped the nails! Then suddenly I felt his grip tighten, saw the muscles of his face begin to twitch as his eyelids fluttered, and I gasped, leaning down towards him as he opened his eyes and saw me.

"Anne." His lips moved, but no sound came. I squeezed his hand and whispered, "Dearest Papa, I am here. Is there anything you want? Shall I send for Mama?"

Again the struggle contorted his features; his blue eyes held mine, their gaze full of urgency.

"What is it, Papa?" I asked more loudly, aware that Mrs Jenkinson had risen and was crossing the room towards us; "Are you in pain? Shall we fetch Dr Harris?"

He moistened his lips with his tongue, and tried again; one word emerged, a hoarse croak: *"Edward."*

"Captain Fitzwilliam will be sent for at once sir," said Mrs Jenkinson quietly, and she exited the room while I raised my father's cold hand to my lips.

"Do you hear that Papa? We have sent for Edward. He will be here very soon. Shall I call Mama?"

But he retreated back into unconsciousness, and spoke no more.

A message was dispatched to Brighton where Edward's regiment was quartered, but we held out little hope of his reaching us in time. We were wrong, however; when he arrived the next morning, wild and disheveled from having ridden all night, Papa still breathed in shallow gasps though his eyes remained closed and his face was now waxy and changed upon the pillow. I whispered that the doctor had made him comfortable, that drugs had been administered, that he was in no pain; and I persuaded my mother to come below and let Edward say his farewells alone.

So it was that Mama and I sat silently in the breakfast room, dry-eyed and exhausted, pretending to pick at the cold repast that had been laid out for us, while Papa breathed his last with Edward at his side. A grey-faced Mrs Henderson brought the message within the hour: the moment had come, had passed, and it was all over.

Later that day – I believe it was the same day – I went looking for my cousin and found him in the library.

"Anne," he said hoarsely as I entered; he rose from his seat at Papa's desk and held out his hand to me. "Thank you," he said, and I responded with equal brevity, "It was his last wish to see you."

Glancing down at an open book upon the desk, I saw my father's handwriting on the flyleaf: *Edouard*, it began, and there followed an inscription in French signed *Louis*, which I did not have time to read before Edward closed the book.

"Did he speak to you at all?" I asked, affecting not to notice; "Did he know you?"

"No words," replied Edward, with visible effort; "But he opened his eyes, and yes, he knew me."

"You must still come often to Rosings," I said later, expanding upon Mama's formal invitation to stay with us until after the funeral; and Edward nodded slowly.

"I shall come every Spring," he said, "and make a tour of the Park. I have promises to keep, you see: I once promised my uncle that if aught were to befall him I would see that no harm came to his cherry trees, his library or his daughter. In that order, pray note. So you will not be able to be rid of me."

We both tried to laugh, though our eyes were glistening; I pressed his hand and left him to his thoughts and his memories, making my way unsteadily along the bleak, empty corridors to my room, suddenly aware of the depth of my fatigue and of the chasm of grief which lay yawning before me.

*****chapter ten*****

I have very little memory of my father's funeral. My main impression is of a room full of people, with Mama in black silk sitting rigidly in Papa's favourite chair at one end and Mrs Henderson ushering in guests at the other. I do remember feeling both surprised and gratified that a quiet, reclusive man like Papa should have attracted so many mourners; not as many as had attended my Uncle Darcy's funeral, but enough to bear witness that he was loved. I know that William was there – I remember seeing him in conversation with Edward, and later with Mama – but I do not recall what I said to him. It was my turn now to be unreachable in grief.

A fortnight or so later, I fell ill. The shock of losing Papa in so sudden and violent a manner, at a time when my nerves were already at full stretch, made me easy prey to a virulent fever which confined me to bed for three full months.

I did not realise until much later how critical was my situation during those months, or how close Mama came to losing a daughter as well as a husband. I remember the pain which racked my limbs, and the burning in my head and throat; Mrs Jenkinson's arm supporting my head as a glass was raised to my lips; the movement of the curtain at the open window and the menacing shadows which danced around the candle during long, broken nights. I recall sharp, vivid dreams invading my sleep with harsh voices and garish colours: my father calling out my name, Miss Harvey's mocking laughter, writhing worms of light, splinters of blue glass. Several times I became aware of a low moaning sound, only to realise as I surfaced from delirium that it came from my own throat. I also have a memory of opening my eyes to find Mama sobbing at my bedside, a sight and sound so startling that I long believed it to have been a dream.

When I came to myself I felt drained, exhausted, and light as a feather. It was a curiously pleasant feeling, as if the flotsam and jetsam of my life had been washed far out to sea, leaving me becalmed upon a wide, white shore. I was horrified, however, upon first seeing my reflection in the glass: I had always been slight and fair-complexioned, but now my face was skull-like and white as bone. My hair came out in great clumps upon the brush, causing me to drop it with a cry of alarm. Mrs Jenkinson was my nurse throughout, singing old lullabies and stroking my head as though I were once again the little girl she had nursed through so many childhood illnesses; and her tender care brought me back to some semblance of health.

"You have nothing to worry about now, my chicken, except regaining your strength. We have all the time in the world. Let me help you to the window, precious – that's right, slowly now, lean upon my shoulder whilst I take your arm. See, I have arranged the cushions nicely for you – let me lift your feet. Now, we must wrap you against the cold – look, the trees are almost bare, just a few bright leaves clinging to the birches. You're as pale and slender as a birch yourself, my poor darling, but have patience – we must all have patience - and we'll have you as bright and gay as a daffodil by Easter."

I was in no hurry whatsoever to be as bright and gay as a daffodil. I had no desire to do anything other than lie upon the sofa and watch the last leaves succumb to their fate, spiraling down one by from the skeletal birches. Every movement pained me and tested my strength. For what seemed like weeks I could walk no further than the window; then gradually I progressed along the length of the corridor outside my room, my knees giving way upon seeing the turn at the landing and the great flight of stairs beneath. Eventually however I was able to descend, and spent a hollow and cheerless Christmas by the drawing room fire, trying to force down sips of spiced wine as the sight of Papa's empty chair brought a lump to my throat. Mama sat watching me anxiously, her voice unusually gentle and low as she read from Georgiana's letter sending me good wishes from herself and William, and promising to visit in the Spring. I felt no enthusiasm at the prospect. I had no wish for company, not even William's; the sensations that his very name had once evoked seemed as distant and ephemeral as a fairy tale. I moved from day to day like one in a dream, feeling quite content to lie upon the couch and watch my life drift by without taking any active part in the proceedings.

It was Edward who first came to visit me, arriving with the crocuses in mid-February. I was reluctant to see him at first, ashamed of my changed appearance and cropped hair; but he wisely persisted, and his company proved to be the restorative I so badly needed. I saw in his face that my pallor and thinness shocked him, but he took my hand with brotherly affection, spoke cheerfully, and declared himself happy to be at Rosings again. We did not speak of Papa at first; in fact I spoke little at all, leaving Edward to manage the conversation. He talked of matters that seemed as distant to me as the moon: his promotion to the rank of Colonel; Georgiana's continued progress at school; William's new London friends, whom he had lately been entertaining at Pemberley.

"He is apparently reckoned to be the perfect host. 'Tis a transformation I should dearly love to witness, should not you, Anne? William making himself agreeable in company – well well! But then a young man in possession of a large estate is always described as the perfect host by guests hoping for a second invitation!"

I tried to smile, but my incomprehension must have shown in my face; Edward looked concerned, and fell silent. At length he said quietly "I am so sorry, Anne, that I had to leave Rosings so soon after – that I could not stay longer, and be more of a help to my aunt and to you. It could perhaps have lessened the gravity of your illness. I have failed in my promise to my uncle."

He blinked rapidly as he spoke, and my desire to reassure him roused me to speech.

"You have nothing to reproach yourself with, Edward; what could you have done? You are a soldier, not a nurse! I think I was better off in the hands of Dr Harris and Mrs Jenkinson, do not you?"

Mama, to do her justice, was both courteous and welcoming to her nephew. Grief had changed her; she had softened towards him, and was appreciative of his kindness to me. Perhaps having now no occasion for jealousy, she could acknowledge his good qualities without rancour; perhaps his promotion to the rank of Colonel impressed her. According to Mrs Jenkinson, Edward was a brave and gallant officer. He must, I realised, be required to command obedience, lead men into danger, risk his life for King and country. William's responsibilities, great as they were, paled into insignificance beside Colonel Fitzwilliam's; and yet Edward gave himself no airs, stood not upon his dignity, remained open and pleasant in his manner to all. Who would not love such a man? Papa, I reflected, would be so proud of him.

The months passed, and I grew stronger. Eventually I became curious to see how Georgiana was getting along, and to feel myself equal to that meeting, both longed for and dreaded, with William. No sooner had I expressed the hope, than Mama arranged the visit. My agitation as the occasion approached was only increased by her repeated assurances that a pale, delicate appearance was greatly preferred by gentlemen of taste, and that short hair was now very much in fashion. I understood fully for the first time that my bloom, such as it was – *'I would not have you lose that delicate bloom, Anne'* - had been irrevocably blighted by my illness; I began to regret having prompted the invitation, which it was now too late to rescind.

The Darcy visit was brief, and every bit as difficult as I feared. William's shock at finding me so changed was obvious for all to see. He recovered his countenance well, quickly replacing his expression of horror with one of concern, but it was too late to erase it from my memory or to prevent me from calculating the implications of it. And it was not just I who had changed. Edward's talk of a 'transformation' had not been exaggerated - Fitzwilliam Darcy was now a man of the world, his manners confident, his appearance fastidious. He spoke, with a detachment that appalled me, of the vulgarity of public balls, the tediousness of dinner parties; of shooting parties organised by a boorish neighbour, Mr Hurst, who had recently married the sister of his friend Charles Bingley; of the merits and shortcomings of Mr Rowe's stewardship; of pressing matters of business at Pemberly, to which he must shortly return.

Was it really less than two years since we had stood beneath the trees in St James' Park, and I had felt myself melt before the eloquence of his gaze? It seemed a lifetime ago. When Mama took him away to make the obligatory call at the Parsonage, leaving Georgiana and I alone together, I felt only relief.

Georgiana was kindness itself, complimenting me upon my hair riband and bringing me extra cushions with sisterly concern. She brought her chair close beside my couch and proceeded to regale me with such tales of school life as had formerly been my delight - but what a chasm now lay between us! Beside Georgiana, I felt old at sixteen; an old maid to whom her eager prattle seemed childish, her robust good looks a reminder of long-faded youth. I reproached myself, recollecting that she had lost both parents, and I only one; but how could I match such resilience? Why was I so damaged, and she so wholesome?

Eventually my listlessness and obvious disinterest defeated her. She timidly observed that I seemed fatigued, and offered to ring for Mrs Jenkinson. I did not object.

When our guests departed on the following day, Mama declared herself vastly pleased with the visit, and with William's solicitude toward me; but I knew otherwise. All my hopes and expectations regarding my handsome cousin were now as insubstantial as a dream. He had left me behind, in a realm of shadow, while he forged his way ahead in the world.

Unequal to battle, I took refuge in surrender; I remained upon the sofa and watched cherry-blossom drift past the window as spring gave way to summer, and my seventeenth birthday came and went.

There was now, of course, no question of my being presented at Court.

*****chapter eleven*****

Another year passed. No doubt my health would have improved more quickly had it not been for the depression of my spirits, which left me with little interest in exercise or study. Mama did not encourage me to exert myself, and Mrs Jenkinson was likewise indulgent; she was getting old, and had every reason for preferring me to take life quietly. The business of rising, dressing and breakfasting would take up the whole of the morning; in the afternoon we would take a modest stroll around the cedar lawn if the weather allowed. We dined early, and spent our evenings at cards if a neighbour could be persuaded to make up a fourth; otherwise I would take up my needlework while Mrs Jenkinson played and sang at the pianoforte, her quavering voice just audible above the tinkle and plod of the keys.

When Edward came at Easter he enticed me into the library, now grown cold and uninviting from long neglect; but I could not or would not make a choice of reading matter, and left to him to select and read from the poets whilst I lay back in my chair and studied the plaster moldings on the ceiling.

Then for my eighteenth birthday I received an unexpected gift: a low phaeton and a pair of dappled ponies stood harnessed and ready in the drive, awaiting my convenience to take a turn around the

Park. Whether Edward had a hand in directing my mother towards this inspired choice I never discovered; but it was just the sort of present Papa might have chosen for me, and proved the very thing to entice me into regular exercise. The earthy scent and warm breath of the ponies instantly recalled the exhilaration of rides around the Park in former days, and soon I was rising earlier, eager to visit the stables and hear their joyful whicker as I approached with apples or sugar. The phaeton was light and easy to handle; it did not take me long to venture beyond the confines of the Park and my daily drives soon took me to Hunsford and beyond, much to the delight of Mama and Mrs Jenkinson whose joy at seeing me in happier spirits touched me deeply, and encouraged me to greater effort.

Occasionally letters arrived from London or Pemberley, full of polite inquiries after my wellbeing; but we received no visit from the Darcys, and Mama was beginning to run out of excuses for her favourite nephew's neglect, and to talk of reprising our annual visit to town to see how her niece got along, when two pieces of news co-incided to involve her more directly in their affairs.

The first came in the form of a letter from Mrs Younge, who throughout my convalescence had remained a faithful correspondent, never once reproaching me for the scant and sporadic nature of my replies. It contained news of greater import than the usual gossip and pleasantries; after three years of marriage, my former governess was now a widow!

A choking fit had apparently been the cause of her husband's demise – the result, I supposed uncharitably, of some over-indulgence at table. It was a remarkably cheerful letter considering the circumstances; it transpired that Mr Younge had left his wife well provided for, and able to realise her 'long-cherished dream' of setting up an establishment for young ladies. She hoped that my mother, as her former employer, would provide her with references, and begged to be remembered to our wider acquaintance, especially those with daughters of suitable age.

It was the first I had heard of this long-cherished dream, but I refrained from pointing this out to Mama who was full of approval for the enterprise and bade me convey, along with her condolences, the assurance of Lady Catherine de Bourgh's full endorsement.

The second piece of news came a fortnight later in a letter from William. Georgiana, he wrote, was soon to leave school, and he and Edward wished to place her with a suitable chaperone so that she might remain in town for the duration of her sixteenth year. Mama, to whom the correspondence was addressed, was now in her element.

"Now this is a handsome letter, Anne," she said handing it over for me to read. "You shall see for yourself how affectionately your cousin asks after you. Of course, he need look no further for an establishment for my niece – I shall recommend Mrs Younge, who will not be averse to confining herself to one charge for a year, especially when she hears who it is to be! I shall write to her at once, and inform her of her good fortune."

"Had you not better first consult William?" I ventured; "He will surely want to discuss the matter with Edward."

"Oh, I shall write to my nephew Darcy of course, but there is no need to involve the Colonel. He will be only too pleased to have the matter settled speedily, and with so little trouble to himself. Now, I may assure your cousin of your good wishes, may I not? He will pleased to hear how your health improves."

Since she was obviously determined to take charge of the situation, I left her to it. I was relieved that she had allowed me to read out the fulsome expressions of gratitude contained in Mrs Younge's recent letter without insisting on perusing it herself; it had contained much gleeful speculation as to the nature and cause of His Majesty's present incapacity, on the grounds of which the Prince of Wales had lately been made Regent. It occurred to me that Mama was not so well placed to recommend Mrs Younge as she imagined herself to be, and I was not at all sure that William would approve the proposal since 'Miss Harvey' had never stood high in his estimation. But I could not wish to deprive Georgiana of the chance to enjoy such vivacious and amusing company as I knew my former governess could provide, nor Mrs Younge of a comfortable income in return for so little trouble. I decided to keep my misgivings to myself, and let fate take its course.

To my astonishment, Mama got her way. To be sure, William expressed the hope that Mrs Younge had acquired steadiness with the marriage state, but he bent surprisingly easily to Mama's persuasion, and the matter was settled within a month. I wondered whether my cousin felt guilty at having neglected us, and hoped by such speedy acquiescence to make amends; as I have already observed, he was not above a little strategy when it came to handling Mama.

Both Edward and Mrs Jenkinson expressed private reservations. The former, when he next came to visit, asked me whether I thought Papa would have approved the scheme, a question I could only answer in the negative. I assured him, however, that Mrs Younge had too much to lose, reputation and income as well as the goodwill of our families, to be anything other than a meticulous chaperone; and since the arrangements had already been made he drew from this what comfort he could, and contented himself with writing to my former governess reminding her of the magnitude of her responsibility.

Mrs Jenkinson remarked several times that a widow was in sole charge of her own reputation, and must be above reproach in all things; I murmured my agreement, knowing that no expression of concern on her part would have any impact in the matter.

In short, to my eternal shame, I ignored my better instincts because I would not give myself the trouble of challenging Mama; and Georgiana, at the age of just fifteen, was placed under the guidance and protection of the former Miss Harvey.

*****chapter twelve*****

No sooner had Mama finished congratulating herself on her excellent management of her niece's affairs than another matter claimed her attention: the task of finding a new incumbent for our little parish church. Our elderly rector, Mr Chisholm, had died following a protracted illness and the curate on loan from Rochester was soon to be recalled. Mama cast around for recommendations, and my Uncle Fitzwilliam suggested a young man, newly ordained and known to the rector at Evesham, who was seeking a living in Kent. Having satisfied herself that he had no leanings of an Evangelical nature (for he was described as being 'very earnest', and she found the Evangelical fervour highly offensive), Mama had him sent for that she might assess his suitability.

I was present at this interview, and I would not have missed it for the world; the man's appearance (his portly torso and thin legs put me in mind of a large, anxious wood pigeon) and manner (he was obsequious in the extreme) combined to make a quite remarkable spectacle. Upon being announced, he entered the room and made a low bow in Mama's direction; then having advanced a few steps he made a second bow in *my* direction, obviously concerned lest I felt myself excluded. When he finally reached us, he bowed twice more with such a smirk upon his face that I could only assume the poor man to be badly afflicted with nerves. I rose and courtesied briefly, resuming my seat as Mama motioned our visitor to the chair upon her left. He seated himself with alacrity and inclined his head expectantly towards her.

"Mr Collins," began Mama without preamble, "I understand that you seek a living in Kent; as you know, our little parish of Hunsford is in need of a pastor. Mr Steele has spoken highly of you to my brother, Lord Amberleigh, and if I consider you to meet the standards of my late husband Sir Lewis de Brough, I shall offer you the living. But firstly I shall require some assurances."

She was about to continue, but Mr Collins seemed unable to contain himself.

"Lady Catherine!" cried he, "Let me assure you that were I to be so fortunate as to be the recipient of your beneficence, I would do all in my power to perform my duties in accordance with your wishes. I would do nothing without first consulting Your Ladyship; I would make no changes, no new arrangement for tithes for example, without first being assured of your Ladyship's approval. It would be my earnest endeavour at all times not only to remember what is due to *you,* but also to encourage such mindfulness amongst my parishioners. I would be ungrateful indeed to embark upon anything without first gaining the approval of so illustrious a patron as yourself."

Mama could hardly believe her luck. Although she was no fool, and could recognise obsequious flattery when she saw it, the advantages of appointing an incumbent so anxious to please her in every way could not be overlooked. With Mr Collins installed at Hunsford, she could continue to hold the absolute sway over parish affairs that Mr Chisolm's age and infirmity had allowed her; and upon Mr Collins her approval was accordingly bestowed. She certainly could not have bestowed it upon a more grateful object!

It was with some curiosity that I accompanied my mother to Church upon the Sunday following our new rector's arrival. If his performance in the pulpit lives up to his performance in the drawing-room, I thought, the good people of Hunsford are in for a more than usually entertaining half-hour! But the sermon he preached was quite unremarkable, distinguished only by frequent bows in the direction of our pew. Mama thought it necessary to invite him to dine with us, if only, I suspected, to ascertain whether the securing of his object would have lessened his desire to flatter. She need not have worried; he accepted with much gratitude, and his conversation was such as I was glad to have witnessed by no-one other than ourselves and Mrs Jenkinson. His attention to me was embarrassing; he could not have been more concerned for my health had he known me all his life, and his attempts to do justice to my beauty whilst acknowledging at the same time how pale and fatigued I appeared were positively Herculean. It was the greatest of pities, he lamented, that I had never been presented: "To have deprived the British Court of its brightest ornament! Fate has been cruel indeed! But rest assured, my dear Miss de Bourgh, that a young lady of such delicate beauty, such excellent accomplishments, needs no introduction to advance her reputation in society. I am sure that wherever you are spoken of, it with the highest admiration."

Mama, knowing as well as I that this was highly unlikely, contented herself with commenting that my health did not allow me to venture often into society, nor to apply myself to those accomplishments at which I could otherwise not fail to excel; thus sparing me the necessity of replying to the compliment, which I was quite at a loss how to do.

Mr Collins was not, it need hardly be said, a regular guest at our dinner table, though he was occasionally invited to make up a number for cards in the evening, and to take supper with us afterwards. I could not but reflect that Papa would have found his conversation insupportable; but Mama was happy to patronise someone so willing to be at her beck and call, and to oblige her I was polite to Mr Collins and sometimes drove to the Rectory in my phaeton bearing a message or packet of comestibles with her compliments. I never set foot in the house however, for I was afraid that once inside the door his effusiveness would make it impossible to leave! Mama could ignore him when she chose to without incurring his offence, and he did whatever she asked of him. She even went to far as to exhort him to marry, and I wondered with amusement how prompt he would be in carrying out her wishes, and how any woman could possibly be persuaded to accept him – for when viewed in a matrimonial light his repulsiveness eclipsed even that of the late Mr Younge.

I took a lively pleasure in describing Mr Collins' antics to Georgiana in my letters; we had re-established a regular correspondence since she had taken up residence with Mrs Younge. Her new establishment suited her, it seemed, very well. Since Mrs Younge was under strict instructions to accept no invitations on her charge's behalf without reference to William or Edward, the concerts and gatherings they attended together afforded only the most respectable society; and my cousin's mentioning that they had more than once encountered George Wickham led me to assume he had found success in his chosen profession and acquired some steadiness of character. They were not to spend the summer in London, it transpired: during August they would come into Kent, and stay a month at Ramsgate. Georgiana promised to send notice of their arrival there, and to visit Rosings with Mrs Younge before they returned to London, a prospect that filled me with joyful anticipation.

When I showed the letter to Mama she immediately took it upon herself to write back with advice about warm wraps and sea breezes, the minimum requirement as to servants, where to change horses, and so forth. She also took pleasure in informing Mr Collins that her niece, Miss Georgiana Darcy, presently established in London under the care of a respectable widow recommended by herself, would be visiting Rosings in August.

"You shall meet them both, Mr Collins," said she, "and you will find Miss Darcy a most elegant young woman; her manners and accomplishments are almost equal to Anne's."

Mr Collins was sure that any niece of Lady Catherine's must indeed be a model of elegance, while at the same time equally sure that no other young lady's accomplishments could equal those of Miss de Bourgh. As I acknowledged his bow with a half-smile, Mama continued: "You may have heard, Mr Collins, of Miss Darcy's brother: my nephew Mr Fitzwilliam Darcy, of Pemberley in Derbyshire."

Mr Collins was delighted to assure her that he had. "He is known to me by repute, your Ladyship. I have always heard him spoken of in the highest terms, as is only to be expected of a relative of the de Bourgh family."

Mama favoured him with a gracious inclination.

"Mr Darcy is not yet married, I believe?"

Ah, now he had touched upon a delicate subject. I bowed my head to hide my blushes while Mama answered smoothly, "Not as yet, Mr Collins; he is but six and twenty, and his responsibilities have come upon him early in life, following the untimely death of my poor brother in law. However, when the time comes" - here she paused to nod significantly in my direction – "he is expected to make a worthy match."

I must surely have looked every bit as appalled as I felt. That Mama, who had never broached the subject of marriage with myself, should now bring up the matter so casually in the presence of an inferior, was mortifying in the extreme; to speak of it as a *fait accompli,* a general expectation, was insupportable! Mr Collins was as delighted as I was horrified.

"A worthy match indeed!" cried he, actually rising from his seat to make a bow in my direction. "A most excellent match, and if I may say so, my dear Lady Catherine, your nephew will be the most fortunate of men!"

My embarrassment was such that I could not acknowledge the compliment, or even meet his eye. My gaze remained lowered for the duration of his interminable call, and by the time he left us I could scarcely contain myself.

"Mama!" I cried reproachfully as soon as the door had closed upon him, "How could you speak so to Mr Collins of William and myself? You know as well as I that we are not engaged; and now Mr Collins – *Mr Collins!* - will consider he has been given *carte blanche* to broadcast my supposed impending marriage all around the parish! Whatever were you thinking of?"

She surveyed me quizzically, her head on one side. "I was thinking, Anne, that it is high time it *was* spoken of. Do not pretend to be in ignorance; I know that your father discussed the subject with you, for he told me of it himself. He also made me promise not to broach the matter until you were at least seventeen, and could decide for yourself how well you liked the idea. Well, I have more than kept my promise, have I not? And you cannot pretend that you dislike your cousin, for I have observed how you look at him and speak of him."

I was shocked into silence. So this was the reason for her reticence – a promise extracted by Papa. The thought of his wanting to protect me from undue coercion brought sudden tears to my eyes; but such misguided optimism could not go unchallenged.

"Dear Mama'" I said at last, in as calm a voice as I could muster, "The observations you refer to date back to before - reflect, Mama, consider – I was but fifteen, it was before – before Papa died, before -"

She remained silent. I tried again.

"Any admiration that William *may* have had for me – any thoughts I may have had of him - it is all changed, Mama, surely you can see that. When he visited us last year he could hardly bear to look at me."

Mama made a sharp, dismissive gesture, as though deliberately slamming the door on any such possibility.

"Nonsense, Anne. You cannot think your cousin so shallow a man as to let a little setback in health undermine his affection? You think him neglectful, no doubt, in not coming oftener to Rosings; but he has duties that keep him occupied both at Pemberley and in town, and cannot always be running down to

Kent. Depend upon it, he will be here next month when my niece visits, and you shall see for yourself that his affection remains unaltered."

I sighed. "William has expressed no particular affection for me – at least, not in words – and since I have been ill -"

"Since you have been ill he has inquired after you most particularly in every letter he writes! My nephew has too much honour, too much pride, to incur the censure of the world and of his family by reneging on his duty, Anne. I shall write to him directly, and request him to visit you – he shall not put it off any longer."

"Mama, I beg you will do no such thing!" I cried, wringing my hands in agitation. "I will not have William summoned to Rosings to be bullied and coerced with talk of duty! Tell me, has he ever given you reason to believe that he actually *wants* to marry me? I have right to ask this, Mama! Pray answer me truthfully."

My mother had the grace to look a little abashed, but she stood her ground.

"Well, he certainly made no demur when his mother and I made our wishes clear to him; why should he?"

"His mother! But my aunt has been dead these seven years and more! How old was William, pray, when this conversation took place?"

"Why, seventeen or thereabouts, I do not recall exactly – old enough to understand what was expected of him, and to know that his mother depended upon his honouring her dearest wish!"

"But Mama," I protested tremulously, "that was nearly ten years ago! You cannot expect a man of nearly seven and twenty, who has lived in the world and formed his own opinions and inclinations, to be bound by a suggestion – an expression of hope, nothing more – made to him as a youth of seventeen! It has to be *his* wish, can you not see that? I will not have it, Mama – if William is to marry me, he has to love me!"

My temples were throbbing, and the tears that I had been determined to hold back spilled hotly from my eyes. Mama rose from her seat in agitation and crossed the room towards me, pausing only to ring the bell for Mrs Jenkinson; she bent over me, patting my hair with awkward tenderness as though soothing a nervous dog.

"My poor child," she murmured, her voice imbued with a sympathy that did nothing to staunch my tears, "I see how it is. You do not wish to enter a loveless marriage. Nor shall you. I would not wish it upon you. But your cousin *does* love you, Anne – he *shall* love you. And he shall prove it to you. He shall come to Rosings, you shall spend time in each other's company, and you shall satisfy yourself that his wishes are in accord with his duty. Ah, Mrs Jenkinson – Miss Anne has the headache, will you be so good as to fetch the eau-de-cologne?"

She continued to stroke my hair at intervals, almost absently, as though deep in thought; when Mrs Jenkson returned with eau-de-cologne sprinkled upon a handkerchief, she murmured in a low voice, "Do not distress yourself, child. It will all come right, I promise you. Leave it all to me."

I watched through a blur of tears as her large, stately figure exited the room. Humiliation, weakness and exasperation mingled with hope as I pressed the cool fragrance to my brow; I wanted so much to believe her.

*****chapter thirteen*****

The month of August came and went with no word from Ramsgate, London or Pemberley. Mama wrote, and wrote again.

"This is strange indeed. What can be the meaning of this silence? I am sure my niece's letter has been misdirected!" were the chief of her comments at first; but as time went by, she grew angry.

"I really think it most ill-mannered of my niece to give us no notice of her arrival in Kent! If their plans had been changed she would surely have informed me – how frustrating this is! We have no address at which to write to *her,* and I had counted upon seeing her at Rosings by now. Mrs Younge must surely realise that their letter has gone astray; she should send an express, or we will have no notice of their arrival. I particularly dislike being kept in ignorance like this! And my nephew is no better – why does *he* not write?"

Mrs Jenkinson and I speculated whether some accident might have befallen the party, and reassured ourselves that had that been the case, word of it must surely have reached us by now. I even wondered briefly – and I was nearer the truth in this than I could possibly have known – whether some romantic entanglement might be claiming Georgiana's attention, rendering her oblivious to family obligations. Mr Bingley, I decided, could be the man – she had mentioned the Bingleys, William's friend Charles and his two sisters, several times in her letters. Mama sent an express to Pemberley asking William to inform us of his sister's whereabouts; but explanation came there none.

Then at the beginning of September came a letter from Edward which threw her into such angry consternation that the entire household soon knew the contents of it.

"Remove my niece from Mrs Younge's care! After less than six months, and with no reason given! What kind of high handedness is this? What can Darcy and the Colonel be thinking of, to do such a thing without consulting me? I shall demand an explanation!"

This she did, and now finally received a reply from Pemberley. No-one was more eager than I to read it, which I did with some trepidation when it was angrily and silently thrust into my hands.

'My dear Aunt,' wrote William, *'Indeed you have not been misinformed by my cousin. My sister has been removed from Mrs Younge's establishment and entrusted to the care of another lady known to my father's family. I am sorry for any displeasure this arrangement may cause you, but it was a joint decision by Colonel Fitzwilliam and myself, and you may rest assured that we have only my sister's best interests at heart.*

'I remain, Madam,
'Your affectionate nephew, &c.'

This was all. No explanation was even attempted, no reference made to the proposed visit to Ramsgate, no apology offered for the long silence over the summer; and the reference to 'another lady known to my father's family' could scarcely have been more insulting to Mama. There were, I noted, no compliments to myself; the tone of the letter was deeply angry, and I was afraid.

Taking my courage in both hands I wrote privately to Georgiana, aware that my correspondence would have to be forwarded from Pemberley but reasoning that William could have no excuse for not doing so. I wrote with careful cheerfulness, saying how surprised I was to hear that she had parted from Mrs Younge so suddenly, and playfully expressing my curiosity to know what adventures had befallen her over the summer.

Georgiana's reply caused me even greater pain than her brother's letter to Mama. 'She was well, she thanked me for my kind inquiries; she had suffered a slight indisposition which had prevented her from seeing us over the summer. She had been sorry to lose Mrs Younge's company but was perfectly satisfied with her new establishment, and with Mrs Annesley.'

It was as though she were writing to another's dictation; indeed I suspected this to be the case. She added that William was now gone into Hertfordshire with Mr Bingley, who had lately taken a house there; and Mama, unable to pursue him with correspondence and incensed at Edward's polite but firm refusal to explain matters more satisfactorily, insisted that I must now write directly to Mrs Younge!

I was most reluctant, as I had by now a deep sense of foreboding about the whole matter. How I longed for Papa's advice! Had he been still with us Edward would surely have told him all, and the crisis could have been smoothed over by now. I did as I was told, and waited wretchedly for several weeks for a reply; by the time Mrs Younge's letter arrived it was nearly December.

She excused the delay by explaining that she had recently changed address, and that my letter had reached her after redirection. She declared herself heartily glad to hear from me, and proceeded to regale me with news from London: had I heard, she wrote, that the Prince of Wales had quarreled with Mr Brummel, and would no longer acknowledge him in public? That the Princess Caroline had taken another lover? That Mrs Fitzherbert had been briefly back in favour with His Highness but was now been demoted yet again in favour of Lady Hertford? At length, she meandered round to the point:

'I was sorry to lose the care of your amiable little Cousin; but it was her brother's decision, and like many great men he seems apt to change his mind when the wind changes direction. I mean no disrespect to your future husband, of course; you will have to learn for your self how best to manage him!

'I have decided not to continue with my establishment, for to own the truth I have had my fill of caring for young ladies; always excepting you, Miss Anne, so do not take it amiss! I have invested Mr Younge's money in this house, and am letting out rooms to lodgers. I am situated right in the centre of town, so as you can imagine I have no shortage of gentlemen seeking accommodation, and can always be sure of keeping up with the latest news!

'Pray give my respectful regards to Lady Catherine, and assure her of my continued gratitude for all that she has done for me.'

And here she signed off, with no reference whatsoever to Ramsgate.

I laid the letter down resignedly, reflecting with shame upon the vulgarity of my correspondent, more apparent to me now than ever before. It confirmed all my worst fears: something had happened which had caused my cousins to question Mrs Younge's character, and remove Georgiana from her influence. For whatever reason, they had no wish to reveal the circumstances and the intimacy between our families had been temporarily suspended.

Poor Mama, I thought as I handed her the letter, not caring what she read or how she now thought of Mrs Younge; William will never come to Rosings now. He will marry someone else and she will have to watch all her plans crumble into dust and see her only daughter end an old maid. I even experienced some perverse satisfaction at the prospect as her outrage washed over me. Taking refuge in fatigue, I retired to my bed and allowed Mrs Jenkinson to fuss over me as much as she wished.

***** chapter fourteen*****

Whilst fretting and fuming over the Darcy family's behaviour, Mama gave vent to her dissatisfaction by interfering further in Mr Collins' affairs. The Parsonage, she declared, was in need of a great many improvements, which only a feminine hand could properly attend to; the kitchen garden was shamefully neglected. Mr Collins was a diligent shepherd to his flock, but his domestic life was in a sorry state; indeed how could it be otherwise, since he lacked a wife? And how was he ever to secure one, since he did nothing to recommend himself to any of the ladies to whom he had been introduced since his arrival at Hunsford? (I can vouch for the truth of this: Mama had invited several respectable spinsters of the parish to take tea with us when Mr Collins was present, and without exception they were appalled at the company they had to endure, and could not escape the experience quickly enough!)

"He does nothing to help himself by conversing with such tortuous pomposity," was Mama's despairing comment. "I am quite at a loss, Anne. Where shall we find a wife for Mr Collins?"

"Could we not just leave him to find his own wife?" I suggested; but she threw up her hands in horror.

"Good heavens, child, that will never do!

Goodness knows what kind of a person he is likely to attract if left to his own devices! For he must have a gentlewoman, you know – I could never countenance anyone other than a gentlewoman at the Parsonage - but she must also be an active, useful sort of person, able to live happily on Mr Collins' income. I have told him all this often enough! But he will never manage it for himself."

Mr Collins, however, was to surprise us all, for he did manage it for himself, and in the following manner.

"I wonder, your Ladyship – I have been intending to ask – might I have leave to visit my cousins in Hertfordshire next month? Of course I would not wish to put your Ladyship to the slightest inconvenience, but I feel -"

"Cousins in Hertfordshire, Mr Collins? What relatives are these, pray?"

"A cousin of my late father, Lady Catherine – a Mr Bennet. A very respectable gentleman by all accounts, though an unfortunate disagreement between him and my father has prevented our becoming acquainted. I am persuaded, however, that enough time has now elapsed for me to offer the olive branch with equanimity; indeed, as a clergyman, I feel honour bound to do so. Mr Bennet has five unmarried daughters, and -"

"Five!" (I silently echoed my mother's exclamation, and sat forward in my chair. This could be interesting.)

"Five daughters! What was the man thinking of?

And all unmarried, you say – pray, what are their ages? And what is Mr Bennet's estate?"

"He is the principal resident of Longbourn, Lady Catherine, a village near the town of Meryton in Hertfordshire. He keeps a very respectable house, I am assured. The youngest Miss Bennet is fifteen, I believe, and the eldest – I am not sure – no older than three and twenty. The estate of Longbourn is – entailed upon myself, in default of any male heir."

Mama was rendered speechless for a moment, and I could not suppress a smile. There was more to our Mr Collins, it seemed, than either of us had supposed.

"Entailed! Upon you! You have never told me, Mr Collins, that you are to inherit an estate! Why, pray, have you never spoken of it before?"

"Well, I – your Ladyship -" stuttered the unfortunate man, "I did not feel it my place – until, that is, I have made my peace with Mr Bennet – I thought it unseemly to presume -"

"Oh, I understand, I understand. No use putting all your eggs in one basket. But this is news indeed! Longbourn, you say, in Hertfordshire; and five daughters of marriageable age! Well, depend upon it, one of them will easily be prevailed upon to accept you, especially as you are to inherit their father's estate. Indeed, they can hardly do otherwise! A very pretty scheme, upon my word! You shall certainly have leave to go, Mr Collins, and I go so far as to charge you expressly not to return until you are an engaged man!"

"You may depend upon it, Anne," reflected Mama when the grateful suppliant had been dismissed and we were able to discuss his prospects in private, "If the Bennet daughters do not have the good sense themselves to look favourably upon Mr Collins, their mother will see to it; she will be a very short-sighted woman if she does not! She has her husband's estate to think of, and her comfort in old age, as well as the possibility that one of so many daughters may end an old maid, and dependent. She will persuade one or other of them to have him, mark my words!"

But when Mr Collins, who always did what Mama required of him, returned from Hertfordshire an engaged man, it was not one of the Miss Bennets who was the chosen partner of his felicity. We were surprised to learn that he had instead secured the eldest daughter of one Sir William Lucas, a neighbour and friend of the Bennet family. This gentleman, though formerly in trade, had been distinguished during his mayoralty of the town of Meryton by a knighthood; and his daughter Charlotte was declared by her enraptured lover to be the most amiable, most accomplished and most virtuous young woman of the neighbourhood. Whether she could possibly be of sound mind was a matter of speculation between myself and Mrs Jenkinson; but this was exactly the kind of wife Mama would have chosen for Mr Collins herself, and once she had got over her astonishment at his not having got one of his cousins, she was all affability and approval, and declared that the wedding must take place as soon as possible.

"Miss Lucas is the eldest daughter of her family, you say? Pray what is her age, Mr Collins?"

"She is seven and twenty, your Ladyship."

"Well! She will not be wanting a long engagement, at seven and twenty! Pray return to Hertfordshire as soon as you like, and arrange the date! And her father is Sir William Lucas, is he? Well, you may tell him from me that he will be most welcome to visit his married daughter whenever he likes, and I will receive him here at Rosings!"

Mr Collins saw nothing untoward in my mother's giving Sir William Lucas permission to visit his own daughter; he was all effusive gratitude, as usual. I was not paying attention to all that he said, for I was wondering whether all five Miss Bennets had refused him in turn, or whether he had become disheartened after one or two rebuttals and decided to look elsewhere. His description of his cousins was uncharacteristically reticent – 'they were most pleasant girls; the eldest was likely to be married quite soon; their father and mother had been most hospitable.' It was not like our Mr Collins to be so economical with words. Something, I suspected, had gone awry in that quarter.

I was aroused from my reverie by the exclamation: "Oh! My dear Lady Catherine, I have omitted to mention a most particular circumstance. Whilst in Hertfordshire I had the pleasure of meeting your nephew – Mr Darcy, of Pemberley!"

I bent my head to avoid the significant glance cast in my direction, while Mama inquired somewhat suspiciously into the circumstances of this meeting.

It transpired that a ball had been given by Mr Bingley at his Hertfordshire residence, to which the Bennets and their guest had been invited. It was there that Mr Collins had encountered William, and taken the liberty of introducing himself – *'taking advantage', as he put it, 'of that privilege which we members of the clergy may claim, in being permitted to lay aside the established forms of ceremony'* – and of assuring him that his esteemed aunt and amiable cousin were both in good health. I was mortified, imagining William's haughty surprise at being thus approached, and was relieved to hear that Mr Collins believed himself to have been received with 'most affable condescension.'

Whilst Mama, her displeasure towards the Darcys temporarily suspended, waxed eloquent upon the impeccable manners of her nephew, I experienced an unpleasant succession of emotions as I pictured a flurry of Miss Bennets, Miss Lucases and other importunate female residents of Meryton all vying for William's attention. The man who had once claimed to find balls so tedious had obviously not been averse to attending this one! And supposing he had already formed an attachment? Mr Bingley's unmarried sister, for instance - how could I have overlooked that possibility? How long would it take Mama to get around to it? I stole an anxious glance in her direction, and was grateful to see that Mr

Collins had the whole of her attention, and that my burning cheeks were safe from scrutiny. I surreptitiously placed a hand upon my heart, in a vain attempt to still its unruly clamour. Accept it, Anne, I told myself; accept the inevitable. Miss Bingley, or someone similar, will soon be mistress of Pemberley.

Mr Collins was married in Hertfordshire early in the New Year, and returned with his bride very promptly to Hunsford to be visited by a great many people, all curious to see how the new Mrs Collins conducted herself. Mama and I were of course among the first to pay our respects, and I was on the whole very favourably impressed. Mrs Collins was plain, neat, and well mannered. She smiled a little too readily, but this could of course be due to nervousness. Her conversation, when her husband's verbosity allowed her to speak, was sensible, desirous to please but not disposed to flatter. Mama seemed likewise well satisfied with her, and invited the happy couple to dine with us the next day.

The Collinses soon became fairly regular guests at our dinner table, being much more welcome as a couple than Mr Collins had been in the single state. Although they were neither lively nor witty company, the husband was often unintentionally amusing and the wife always pleasant and friendly. I began to admire Mrs Collins for the diplomatic way in which she handled her husband, and for the equanimity with which she bore my mother's interference into every aspect of her domestic affairs.

Her age and situation, I decided, were sufficient explanation for her having accepted Mr Collins' proposal; and if she did not show much obvious affection for him, neither did she betray any repugnance or regret. She seemed cheerfully determined to make the best of her situation, and I could only wish her well.

*****chapter fifteen*****

The first signs of Spring were beginning to refresh the sparse winter verdure of the Park when Mr Collins announced that his father-in-law, his sister-in-law and one of his cousins were coming to spend a few weeks at the Parsonage. Mama, who had long been curious to meet Mrs Collins' family, was quick to approve the visit and to assure him of an early invitation for the whole party to wait upon us. Initially, I was a little put out by the news: this incursion of Lucases might coincide with Edward's Easter visit, during which I was planning to wheedle from him the particulars of Georgiana's removal from Mrs Younge. It was a task that would require both tact and privacy, and any extra demands upon our hospitality might diminish the opportunity for private conversation. I could not deny, however, that I also was curious to see what manner of man was Sir William Lucas; and more particularly, I was curious to meet one of the Bennet sisters – for the cousin, Miss Elizabeth Bennet, was apparently the second eldest, and Mrs Collins' particular friend.

Accordingly I was happy to oblige Mama when news of their arrival reached us by driving to the Parsonage in my phaeton with Mrs Jenkinson, bearing the promised invitation to dine with us the next day. Mr Collins, all bows and smiles, begged me to step inside and meet his guests, but the sight of a second large gentleman bowing and smiling in the doorway, whom I took to be Sir William Lucas, made me fear such a resemblance between father- and son-in-law as could not be tolerated in a confined space. I softened my refusal by engaging Mrs Collins in conversation for a while, expressing pleasure in her happiness at receiving her family into her home and in the prospect of receiving them into ours on the morrow.

The requirements of civility having been fulfilled, Mrs Jenkinson and I took our leaves and continued our drive; but not before I had observed two faces watching us from the Parsonage window. One, pale and neat, a younger and prettier Mrs Collins, must of course be Miss Maria Lucas; the other, vivacious and shrewd-looking, with lively dark eyes and chestnut curls, must equally obviously be Miss Elizabeth Bennet. I was a little put out to observe that she stared at me openly, and made what appeared to be amusing comments to her companion; my initial impression was less than favourable.

We dined unfashionably early at Rosings – five o'clock was my mother's favoured hour – and our guests, obviously primed by the Collinses, arrived in good time. Sir William, whom I had feared might be as verbose as his son-in-law, was at first remarkably silent; a low bow was his only response to Mama's greeting, and he took his seat with ponderous gravity. During dinner, however, he recovered the power of speech and employed it to no better end than to echo every sentiment expressed by his son-in-law. Mr Collins found it necessary to rhapsodise over every dish as it was presented, and to hear such a pompous and substantial-looking gentleman as Sir William Lucas rhapsodising likewise was almost as amusing as it was irritating. Miss Elizabeth Bennet, who was seated next to me, was certainly diverted; several times I observed her raise her napkin to hide her smile, and once or twice she looked sideways at me to observe how I kept my countenance. I avoided her eye and took my cue from Mama, whose good breeding enabled her to receive this double flow of compliments with equanimity. I did pity Mrs Collins, who made several attempts to divert our attention from the absurdities of her husband and father. Miss Lucas I also felt sorry for – she seemed extremely shy, and uttered not one word during the whole course of the meal. I thought it safest to confine my conversation to Mrs Jenkinson.

When we escaped from the gentlemen to the refuge of the drawing-room, I looked forward to hearing a little more from Miss Lucas and Miss Bennet than had hitherto been possible. Miss Bennet's vivacious manner earned her pride of place next to Mama; she accepted the proffered seat with alacrity, having no idea what was in store! Mama subjected her to a veritable interrogation, and for once I was grateful for the thoroughness of her inquiries since they enabled me to satisfy my own curiosity by proxy.

"You are the second eldest of your family, I

believe, Miss Bennet; pray, what are the names of your sisters? Is it true that the eldest is soon to be married?"

Miss Bennet's initially confident expression was swiftly replaced by one of alarm. "It is not true, ma'am, I assure you," was her quick response. "My elder sister Jane is staying with my uncle and aunt in London at present. She is *not* engaged to be married; I wonder where your Ladyship can have heard such a rumour?"

In the absence of Mr Collins, Mama shot an accusing glance towards his wife before continuing smoothly, "And the younger Miss Bennets? What of *their* prospects? Are any of them reckoned to be pretty?"

Miss Elizabeth inclined her dark head archly and appeared to give the matter some thought. "My youngest sister Lydia is reckoned to be extremely pretty; but neither she, Mary nor Catherine have any marriage prospects at present."

"Well!" said Mama, "That is a great pity, since I understand your father's estate to be entailed upon Mr Collins. Of course I am glad of that for *your* sake, Mrs Collins, but in general I see no reason for entailing estates away from the female line. It was not thought necessary in Sir Lewis de Bourgh's family!"

I reflected that this was just as well, since there were no male de Bourghs left in England and Rosings would pass to some obscure French cousin, which would be problematical in the present climate.

I wondered whether Papa would have thought it prudent, under such a circumstance, to name Edward as his heir after all; in which case Mama might have deemed it more convenient for me to marry *him*. I remembered my conversation with Papa in the library all those years ago; how he had championed my right to marry whomsoever I chose but had been unable to explain to a ten-year-old child why a man of Edward's inclination would not make an ideal husband. Then I realised with a pang that the absence of an entail would make little difference, since I was to end an old maid and Rosings would probably fall to the French after all.

This mental detour prevented my discovering what kind of carriage Mr Bennet kept, and what was Mrs Bennet's maiden name; but I recovered my attention in time to learn that the Miss Bennets had all been educated at home without a governess, and that in spite of the youngest being but fifteen they were all out in society, which Miss Elizabeth declared boldly to be only fair, seeing that the elder sisters had neither the means nor the inclination to marry early.

Mama, who was used to a greater degree of deference, remarked tartly that Miss Bennet gave her opinion very decidedly for so young a woman. I was inclined to agree; her pertness was beginning to grate upon me.

"Do you play and sing, Miss Bennet?" was Mama's next question, and Miss Elizabeth's reply, though modestly phrased – "Only a little, ma'am" – was accompanied by such a confident glance towards the instrument and obvious preparation to rise and take her place there, that I was pleased to see her expectation snubbed by Mama's merely commenting that we should be happy to hear her at some time or other.

When the gentlemen joined us we drank tea, and then proceeded to cards. Miss Bennet and Miss Lucas joined Mrs Jenkinson and myself for cassino, whilst Mama commandeered the gentlemen and Mrs Collins for quadrille. Miss Bennet was so obviously put out by this arrangement, and Miss Lucas so shy and unequal to conversation, that we all restricted our comments to the matter in hand; and by the time we had dealt only a couple of rounds Miss Elizabeth was beginning to gape. I concluded that she had no liking for cards, and was used to livelier pastimes: dancing, for instance, at Hertfordshire balls hosted by accommodating neighbours. I reflected with chagrin that she must find me very dull. When Mama finally sent for the carriage to convey our guests back to the Parsonage, the relief, for our table at least, was mutual.

*****chapter sixteen*****

Sir William Lucas, we learned, was to stay only a week at Hunsford. We saw him just once more before his departure, and since his behaviour on that occasion was exactly the same as before I did not regret the loss of his company. Miss Lucas and Miss Bennet, however, were to remain at the Parsonage for several weeks, and for them Mama had news which she knew could not fail to impress.

We had heard from Edward at last, and his letter gave notice not only of his own arrival at Rosings in time for Easter, but of William's accompanying him for the whole of the visit! This was unexpected, and Mama and I were thrown into a flurry of anticipation. In Mama's case, the anticipation was solely pleasurable; she was convinced that William had seen the error of his ways and wished to make a personal apology for his offhand behaviour over the summer. My own was not unmixed with dread; my mother would certainly demand a full explanation for Georgiana's removal from Mrs Younge's care, and if the one proffered proved unsatisfactory would worry away at the subject like a dog with a bone until all of William's goodwill evaporated and the situation was worse than ever. I was heartily glad that Edward would be with us, for his diplomatic skills would be sorely needed.

I had quite forgotten that both Miss Bennet and Miss Lucas had already made William's acquaintance in Hertfordshire. Miss Elizabeth made it clear that this had been no passing introduction: she and her sister Jane, she said, had spent several days at Netherfield Hall, Mr Bingley's residence, as guests of the Bingley sisters while William was staying there; she had also encountered him at various private parties, and on one occasion had even danced with him!

"He asked me to dance only once," she laughed, "but I was assured that it was a very great honour, for he is known to dislike the amusement in general; or at least, he is known to dislike it in Hertfordshire!"

Mama was much put out by this flippant attitude. "Mr Darcy," she declared sternly, "is a gentleman who expects the same high standards of his acquaintance as of himself. He would not dream of giving consequence to undeserving young women; you may certainly believe that his asking you to dance was a very great compliment indeed."

Miss Bennet looked almost satirical as she replied, "I am sure that it was, Lady Catherine." She cast a sideways glance at me, to see no doubt how I liked the idea of my cousin having paid her this very great compliment. I did not like it at all, but was at pains to appear indifferent; and my mortification was only increased by Mama's emphasising that her nephew Darcy had a special attachment to Rosings, and that although Miss Bennet would no doubt be seeing him in due course he would wish to confine himself to the family circle for the first few days.

By the day of my cousins' arrival, I was in a fine state of nerves. Mama insisted that I remain upon the sofa as the gentlemen were shown into the room, and I received them with such a mixture of pleasure and trepidation as would have been impossible to hide had I been required to rise and courtesy. Edward was all ease and kind solicitude as usual; William, though he said all the right things, was neither. He looked much the same - his jaw was perhaps a little squarer and his hair cut shorter - but his manner was too guarded, his address too formal. His dark gaze slid away from my face, and he would not meet my eye. I inquired after Georgiana; he replied that she was well. I mentioned that I had not heard from her in a while; he assured me that she had every intention of writing soon. I felt the tears well up as I resigned him to Mama, and was glad that her monopoly of both our guests left my struggle unobserved.

My mother had wisely decided against broaching the subject of explanations and apologies at this first meeting, and I was thankful to observe her make herself equally welcoming to both her nephews.

"You have already made the acquaintance of our new rector I believe, Darcy; Mr Collins is quite a character, is he not? He is most obliging, but I find a little of him goes a long way. His wife is a pleasant enough young woman – you know her from Hertfordshire, I think – and her sister Miss Lucas is staying with them at present, along with Miss Elizabeth Bennet who also claims an acquaintance with you. Fitzwilliam, I thought you would do for her, when next we invite them to Rosings – you know, talk to her, accompany her to the pianoforte and suchlike. She likes to talk, and express her opinions. Darcy can have Miss Lucas - she is more reserved, and will allow Anne her share of the conversation."

Because I was observing William's face, I could not miss the astonishment which suffused his countenance upon hearing the names of the Parsonage guests. "Miss Elizabeth Bennet?" he echoed in tones of disbelief. Mama did not notice; she was responding to Edward's inquiry, confiding that Miss Bennet seemed a pretty, genteel sort of girl on first acquaintance, but there was a boldness about her that was quite unbecoming – the result, she opined, of her having been allowed to run quite wild at home, since her parents had been sadly neglectful of their daughters' education. William, when applied to, would neither confirm nor deny this: Mr Bennet, he said, 'was a very respectable gentleman'; and whilst admitting that 'the younger Miss Bennets were perhaps a little lively' he declared firmly that 'the eldest Miss Bennet and her sister Miss Elizabeth were generally much admired'. He seemed greatly put out by this unexpected re-encounter with people he thought to have left in Hertfordshire, and Mama took pains to assure him that the guests at the Parsonage would not be intruding upon our family circle over the Easter period.

Georgiana's change of situation was finally

discussed after dinner, and thanks to Edward's calm and placatory answers to my mother's questioning was resolved without any of the recrimination I had been dreading. An unseasonal cold, he explained, had prevented our cousin from making the trip to Ramsgage; and Mrs Younge, instead of informing us as she had been requested to do, had made use of the summer season to advance her own business interests in London, viz. the purchase of the lodging house over which she now presided. This amounted to such a flagrant breach of duty as to leave William and Edward little choice but to remove their ward from her care. The fact that we had not been kept informed of these events had been overlooked in the ensuing upheaval and search for an alternative establishment, and an unreserved apology was now offered by Edward and echoed by a stony-faced William. The mere mention of Mrs Younge's name seemed to cause him agitation, and I felt guilty once again for not speaking out about the flaws in her character. Mama, whose opinion of her former employee had already been lowered by the contents of her final letter, seemed content to lay the matter to rest, even grudgingly admitting that 'we had all been much deceived in Mrs Younge.'

I was not so easily satisfied, however. The inexplicable brevity and coldness of both William's and Georgiana's letters remained unexplained – replies so reluctantly given after so many requests were surely not attributable to 'oversight.' In addition, I could tell from Edward's manner that he was uncomfortable with the explanation he had been obliged to give; he was concealing or falsifying something, I was sure of it. William said as little as possible, and I though badly of him for not shouldering his share of the burden. I reluctantly decided against trying to force Edward's confidence in private; curious though I was, I did not wish to cause him further distress.

On the morrow, Mr Collins came to pay his respects and I was pleased to see my cousins receive him with civility, William being prepared for his idiosyncrasies by prior acquaintance, and Edward by advance warning. I was surprised, however, to hear William offer to accompany him back to the Parsonage to wait upon the ladies. Edward seemed likewise taken aback, but was ready to oblige, saying to me in a low voice, "It is only right that we pay our respects to Mrs Collins; and I must say, Anne, my aunt's description of her guests has made me curious to meet them also."

"Upon my word," cried Mama when they were gone, "That was hardly necessary! What think you, Anne? But then Darcy is always so attentive to these things. No doubt he felt he could not do otherwise, being already acquainted with them. Well, at least it excuses us from having to invite them here for a while! We may safely leave *that* for a few more days, and have the gentlemen to ourselves."

We did indeed pass a pleasant week *en famille* with my cousins; far pleasanter, in fact, than I could have envisaged. The addition of two young gentlemen to our card table enlivened our evenings considerably, and I enjoyed driving Edward round the Park in my phaeton. He seemed pleased with the diversion which the Collinses and their guests supplied: "I find Mrs Collins very amiable," said he, "though her husband tries one's patience sorely, and one can scarce get a word out of her sister! Miss Bennet, on the other hand, is easy to converse with. She *is* rather high-spirited, and I can see why you find her vivacity a little overwhelming; but I did not detect any actual vulgarity, and at least she does not flirt! At any rate, she seems pleasant enough, and I shall call again when I have the opportunity – would you care to accompany me, Anne? No, I see you would not. My poor little cousin – you have become unused to company, but it would do you good, you know, to step back into society. I should dearly love to see you dance again! You are so much improved since last I saw you, and – oh look, Anne, the daffodils! Like a carpet of gold beneath the cedars – do you remember when we picked enough to fill two great vases?"

I laughed, embarrassed to think of our conversation all those years ago: – *'I thought everyone had to get married, Edward...' 'Well, it is not yet enshrined in English law!'*

I was pleased that Edward found me much improved, for William seemed to think me still an invalid. He made no effort to draw me out in conversation, or to entice me out of doors. He was perfectly polite, but had little to say to me even when we were alone together – a circumstance which my mother was at pains to contrive. Poor Mama – my heart went out to her even as her blind and dogged optimism exasperated me. Whenever I caught her eye, she would smile and nod encouragement; she was honouring her promise not to broach the subject of marriage until William he had declared his affection for me, an eventuality which seemed increasingly improbable as the days progressed.

It was Edward who prompted Mama to invite the Collinses to Rosings; he was anxious to fulfil the obligations of politeness, and mindful that the invitation was overdue. Mama's feathers were somewhat ruffled; she declared that if he enjoyed Miss Bennet's company so much he must engage to entertain her for the evening.

"I will do my best, ma'am," was Edward's mild reply.

Accordingly, when we attended Church on Easter Day Mama complimented Mr Collins on his interminable sermon and informed him that we would be happy to receive him, his wife and their guests after dinner that evening. I was relieved that they had not been invited to dine; it meant we would have to endure less of Mr Collins' conversation, and could anticipate the visit as a welcome diversion at the end of the day.

When our guests arrived and joined us in the drawing room, Edward obligingly seated himself next to Miss Elizabeth and engaged her in conversation; but Mama was by then in so contrary a mood that she kept calling over to ask what they were talking of.

"We are talking of music, ma'am," said Edward patiently; upon which she cried, "Then pray speak aloud, so that Anne and I may have our share of the conversation! You know how greatly I love music. If I had learned to play, I should have been a great proficient; as would Anne, had her health allowed her to practise. Darcy, how does your sister get on with her music?"

"She is wonderfully proficient, madam," replied William with fraternal pride; and when Mama exhorted him to encourage Georgiana to practise regularly he retorted sharply, "I assure you ma'am, my sister needs no encouragement; she practises most assiduously."

Somewhat taken aback by his tone, Mama turned to Miss Bennet and issued an ill-advised invitation to avail herself of Mrs Jenkinson's pianoforte whenever *she* wished to practise; adding that 'she would be in nobody's way in that part of the house.' An awkward silence fell. I was mortified, as always when Mama gave unwitting offence, and not even Mrs Jenkinson's assurance that Miss Bennet would be welcome to her pianoforte at any time elicited a response from that young lady, who was obviously determined to repay rudeness in kind.

It was left to poor Edward to smooth things over, which he did in the most appropriate way possible: he requested Miss Bennet to play and sing for us after coffee, and when the time came accompanied her to the instrument and pulled up a chair that he might give her performance his full attention. I hoped this would make amends for Mama's clumsiness, and was soon listening with pleasure to Miss Bennet's performance; her voice, though not strong, was tuneful and pleasing, her touch upon the keys both confident and light. I ventured a few words to Mrs Collins in praise of her friend, while Mama made some comment to William. What she said to displease him this time I do not know, but he actually got up and walked away from her, approaching the pianoforte and attaching himself to Edward and Miss Bennet, who broke off her performance to talk to him. Before long all three were engaged in animated conversation, laughing together without a thought for the rest of us and pointedly ignoring Mama's interruptions. It was only when she rose and approached them herself that Miss Bennet resumed playing.

When she had finished we applauded politely, and Mama grudgingly praised her fingering; though she could not refrain from adding that Miss Bennet's taste in music was not equal to mine, a remark which completely annulled the compliment and brought a flush of embarrassment to my cheeks.

For the best part of an hour, Miss Elizabeth continued to play and sing, encouraged by both William and Edward, and I was in the throes of torment; nothing, it seemed, had prepared me for the experience of observing my cousins enjoy the company of another woman at the pianoforte! I was thoroughly ashamed of such petty jealousy, but my sensibilities seemed impervious to reason. When at last the carriage was ordered I could scarcely look at Miss Bennet as I bade her farewell, and the supercilious air with which she made her courtesy without wishing me good night convinced me that she cared naught for my feelings or my good opinion. I felt that I had unwittingly made her my enemy, though I had no idea how.

All in all the evening consisted of one faux pas after another, and when it was over I retired miserable to bed where I disgraced myself still further by retreating into babyhood and crying myself to sleep.

*****chapter seventeen*****

Next morning William went out by himself, and Edward, seeing me in low spirits, offered to accompany me on my drive around the Park. I assented gladly, for I needed someone to talk to; and when, after a little distance, we stopped to watch the dance of the daffodils I asked him whether he thought Mama had given lasting offence to our guests last night. He laughed it off.

"Oh Anne, 'tis no matter, think nothing of it! The Collinses must be well used to my aunt's manner by now, and as for Miss Bennet and Miss Lucas – well, they are the Collinses' guests, not yours, and in a fortnight or so they will be gone. They are pleasant enough girls, but *you* owe them nothing Anne – you do not need their good opinion."

"I know I do not *need* it, but I should like to have it all the same! Miss Bennet is so superior, with her witty conversation and her confidence and skill upon the instrument -"

"Superior? Oh come now! Socially, she is very much your inferior and has only her wit to recommend her – you cannot envy her, surely?"

"I do not envy her situation, of course," I responded thoughtfully, "but I do envy her confidence, her ability to play and sing and amuse everybody. *You* found her society pleasing – oh cousin, do not look at me so, I meant no pettiness – I only meant that I wish I could be more lively in company myself. After an evening in Miss Bennet's society I feel so dull by comparison."

Edward took my hand, and was silent for a while. I began to feel thoroughly ashamed of myself; but then he said, "Dear Anne, listen to me. You have been ill, and even if that were not the case, it is not in your nature to prattle and tease. Were you to to affect it, it would be as unbecoming as a facade of hauteur would be to Miss Bennet. Her manners are naturally vivacious and provocative – yours are gentle and sincere. You are both being yourselves, there is nothing to compare or judge. People are different, Anne." He patted my hand, adding *sotto voce* "The world would be a happier place, I think, if we could just accept the simple fact that people are different."

I squeezed his hand in gratitude; my feelings would not allow me to speak. After sitting in companionable silence for a while we continued our drive, overtaking William on our return as he approached the house on foot.

"Darcy!" called Edward as we slowed to greet him, "Where have *you* been this morning? We have been all round the Park, and no sign of you!"

"I walked to the village," he replied calmly, "and called at the Parsonage on my way back; but excepting Miss Bennet they were all out, so I did not stay long."

"We will see you back at the house then," said

Edward; and as we drove on he remarked, "There, you see, Anne – our cousin has already paid off any arrears of civility incurred last night."

In the drawing room that evening, the sight of the pianoforte caused Mama to revive the subject of Elizabeth Bennet.

"I thought she performed for us *quite* well," she said, "but I have no wish to encourage her further. Apart from anything else, it is unfair to Anne. You should have thought of that, Fitzwilliam, before urging her to play for us."

"Indeed, ma'am," replied the long-suffering Edward, "I would not distress Anne for the world; but I honestly thought Miss Bennet's playing and singing would entertain us all."

"I assure you, Mama," I interjected hastily, "there is no need for anyone to feel concerned on my account. I enjoyed Miss Bennet's performance very much – I told Mrs Collins how much I enjoyed it. And you did specifically request Edward to engage and entertain her, a duty he discharged with much kindness and gallantry."

"H'mm," said Mama grudgingly, obviously put out with both her nephews for having taken pleasure in a tiresome social duty; "He was certainly most attentive. And you, Darcy, should have confined yourself to Miss Lucas. I am sure she felt herself quite neglected. There was no need for *both* of you to dance attendance upon Miss Elizabeth Bennet – who knows what inflated opinion of herself your flattery may have aroused? I am thinking particularly of *you*, Fitzwilliam," – turning back to Edward – "for I hear that you have been calling at the Parsonage often, and alone. I hope you have not given her the wrong idea!"

There was a short, uncomfortable silence. Even William looked horrified.

"I assure you, ma'am," said Edward carefully, "that nothing could be further from my intentions. I have merely been following the dictates of neighbourliness, as I'm sure my uncle would wish me to do. Why Darcy, you called upon Miss Bennet alone just this morning, and no-one thought anything of it, I'm sure!"

"Well of course nobody *here* suspects you of harbouring intentions, Fitzwilliam," rejoined Mama impatiently, "But *she* may have gained the wrong impression. Girls in her position will jump at anything these days."

Edward started to laugh, and looked to William to join him – but to his astonishment and mine, William solemnly concurred with Mama.

"It might be as well to make yourself clear, Fitzwilliam," he said seriously. "I think Miss Bennet does find your company a little too agreeable. It would be unfortunate indeed if she had formed any expectations."

Poor Edward was at first too astonished to reply; but observing that his cousin seemed quite in earnest, he finally said in quiet, clipped tones, "Very well, Darcy, if you really think it necessary."

His offence and displeasure were evident, and I

felt for him, felt all the outrage of such an attack upon his integrity. When, to on-one's surprise, he abruptly left the room, I turned accusingly upon William, made bold in the face of injustice.

"Was it really necessary to speak so to Edward, cousin?" I asked; "Miss Bennet can surely not have formed any designs upon him in so short a space of time; even if she were tempted to misread his kindness, she must surely realise that his supposed admiration cannot lead to anything serious. Reflect, consider, and you will see how unlikely such an imputation must be."

William had the grace to look a little abashed, but persisted in his opinion. "We cannot afford to be sanguine in these matters, Anne; such unequal matches take place all the time. And yes, Fitzwilliam *will* be expected to marry at some stage, and he will wish to do it with as little trouble to himself as possible. Marrying beneath his station in life would be one way to secure an undemanding wife."

I was so taken aback by such frankness that I knew not how to reply! When Mama, also much surprised, asked with asperity why William supposed Miss Elizabeth Bennet would make an undemanding wife, he finally did appear ashamed; mumbling that he had only wished to make a general point he quickly turned the conversation, much to my relief.

*****chapter eighteen*****

My cousins were due to leave us at the end of the week; but to my surprise, they were easily prevailed upon to extend their visit by several days, with William seemingly the more anxious of the two to accede to Mama's invitation! She of course chose to see this as a compliment to me, but I knew otherwise and was extremely puzzled. Not once had William sought my company, encouraged my conversation or paid me any particular compliment; in fact he had seemed preoccupied and distant since the moment of his arrival, never offering to take Edward's place beside me in the phaeton but preferring to walk the Park alone. I was at a loss to account for his continued presence with us, though glad to have Edward at Rosings a little longer.

Two days into their extended stay, Edward entered the drawing room where William and I were sitting – William engrossed in the newspaper, and I occupied with my needlework – with the following cheerful announcement: "You may congratulate yourself, Darcy, on having prevented yet another imprudent marriage! I have just encountered Miss Elizabeth Bennet quite by chance in the Park, and took the opportunity to make it perfectly clear that I have no intention of proposing to her. It was all most discreetly done, I assure you. You may express your approval, if you like."

Mama was not present to conduct an interrogation, but William looked uncomfortable, as well he might; he hastily folded the newspaper and sat back in his chair. "What did you say to her?" he asked warily.

"Oh, I merely commented that younger sons cannot afford to marry anyone they happen to like. Or words to that effect."

"Well, that was hardly discreet! What said Miss Bennet?"

"She said, *'unless they like women of fortune, which I think they often do!'* That was astute, was it not? I really do not think she will be pining for me."

William seemed to find this both pleasing and amusing. He rose and strolled over to the window, smiling to himself, while I begged an explanation from Edward as to what he meant by 'yet another imprudent marriage'.

"Oh, Bingley," he replied airily; "At least I *assume* it was Bingley – Darcy, will you not confirm for us that it was Charles Bingley you referred to when you said you had advised a friend against an imprudent marriage?"

I turned questioningly to William and he did confirm it, though without further elaboration.

"And who was the lady?" I pressed, eager for details.

"No-one you would know, Anne. A Hertfordshire acquaintance."

"And why would it have been an imprudent marriage?"

"The usual reasons: vulgar connections, an unsuitable family – the lady herself was pleasant enough. Excuse me, Anne – Fitzwilliam – I believe I must speak to my aunt." He bowed perfunctorily in my direction, and made towards the door.

"Well, Miss Bennet seems to think your interference in the matter unnecessarily officious," commented Edward with a shrug, picking up the newspaper and preparing to occupy the chair that our cousin had just vacated. William froze abruptly in mid-stride, and wheeled around with an expression horror on his face.

"Miss Bennet? You mentioned the matter to her? By what right? What on earth possessed you to speak of such a thing?"

Edward and I were equally astonished, and he not a little annoyed. "For heaven's sake Darcy!" he retorted, "Am I now not allowed so much as a word of conversation without your permission? Yes, I mentioned the circumstance to Miss Bennet, as an example, if you must know, of the constancy of your friendship. I was speaking in praise of you; but I will save myself the trouble in future!"

Now, I thought, William must surely apologise; but instead he persisted with his questioning.

"Did you mention Bingley by name? Did you speculate as to the identity of the lady involved?"

"Yes, I mentioned Bingley by name. No, I did not speculate about the lady; why on earth would I? I have no idea who she is! Now, if you will allow me, Darcy, I should like to read my newspaper in peace!"

And Edward sat himself down in high dudgeon, unfolded the broadsheet and left William to wander distractedly from the room.

I remained in my seat, lost in silent speculation as to the cause of his discomposure. The unsuitable lady, I surmised, must be a mutual acquaintance, though why Miss Bennet's knowledge of Willliam's involvement should agitate him so I could not imagine. There was more to his interest in Charles Bingley's affairs than he was willing to disclose; could he perhaps be hoping to secure his friend for Georgiana? I dwelt long upon this possibility, which fitted neatly with another that I had already considered, viz. William's own plans regarding the unmarried Bingley sister, Miss Caroline. If Charles Bingley were to marry William's sister, might he not feel obliged to be punctilious in returning the compliment? Could he even now be speaking to Mama, releasing himself from his supposed obligation to me? Was that why he had prolonged his visit? If so, we were in for an uncomfortable evening, especially as the Collinses and their guests had once more been invited to drink tea with us!

The evening arrived, however, without my having observed any ill humour between William and Mama; I concluded that I had either been precipitous in my surmise, or that William, for whatever reason, was biding his time.

When our guests arrived, I found myself greeting only the Collinses and Miss Lucas; Miss Bennet, it transpired, was indisposed with a headache and sent her apologies. I was initially disappointed, having planned to scrutinise her manner towards Edward; it occurred to me that his declaration of disinterest might have disappointed her more than he supposed.

Mama was extremely put out – she did not much like Miss Bennet, but expected her to attend upon us when invited to do so, and now Mrs Jenkinson must be called upon to make up the numbers for cards. William seemed likewise put out, inquiring most particularly into the severity of Miss Elizabeth's headache as though he also suspected her of shamming.

The visit progressed well enough however; without Miss Bennet to dominate the conversation I actually managed to engage Miss Lucas, and discovered her to be, beneath her shy exterior, a pleasant and intelligent girl. When tea was over we prepared for cards, and I hardly noticed when William excused himself and left the room.

As the minutes passed, however, his absence began to impinge upon us and at length Mama sent a servant to inquire for him. He was not in his room; and it soon transpired that late as the hour was, he had gone out – alone, on foot, and without explanation! Mama excused his rudeness to our guests as best she could, though her displeasure was evident for all to see; and eventually she made up a table with Edward, Mr Collins and Miss Lucas, leaving Mrs Collins, Mrs Jenkinson and myself to occupy ourselves as we pleased.

It was a fine May evening, and I chose to take a

book to the window seat while the other two conversed alone. There was plenty of light still to read by, but I could not keep my mind upon the page for speculating about my cousin's strange behaviour and current whereabouts. Nor could I help overhearing Mrs Collins and Mrs Jenkinson, who were speculating likewise.

"It is most unlike Mr Darcy," Mrs Jenkinson was saying, "to leave so suddenly, and with no explanation to Lady Catherine. I thought at first that he had been taken ill; but if that were the case he would not have gone out. I do hope he has not received distressing news! But no message has arrived this evening, and if anything of import to the family had occured Lady Catherine and the Colonel would have been likewise informed. 'Tis all very strange – do you not think so, Mrs Collins?"

Mrs Collins concurred. "It is certainly most strange. He cannot have gone further than the village on foot; but who could he possibly be calling on so late? We are all here excepting Miss Bennet, and he knows her to be indisposed."

We are all here excepting Miss Bennet. I was just suppressing a gape when the jolt shot through me, rendering me fully awake as the scales finally fell from my eyes. Miss Caroline Bingley, forsooth! How could I have been so blind?

'Such unequal matches take place all the time'. 'It would be as well to make yourself clear, Fitzwilliam - I think Miss Bennet does find your company a little too agreeable'. 'You have mentioned this to Miss

Bennet? By what right? Did you speculate as to the identity of the lady involved?'

Oh yes, I echoed silently, grimly exultant, it is certainly most strange that Fitzwilliam Darcy should be so very concerned as he seems to be about the inclinations, opinions and matrimonial prospects of *Miss Elizabeth Bennet.*

*****chapter nineteen*****

And so it was that I knew, months before the event, that a crisis loomed that would rock the relationship between Rosings and Pemberley to its foundations. Everything that happened subsequently, all that I am about to relate, I was able to observe from a lofty and privileged perspective; because ever since that May evening when Miss Bennet excused herself from our company on account of a headache and William left the house without explanation, I knew. My cousin's discomposure upon hearing her name, his extraordinary concern about Edward's making himself 'too agreeable', his surprising eagerness to extend his visit, all made sense in the light of one simple fact: he was in love with Elizabeth Bennet.

And of course, I said nothing. Why should I? I had long been persuaded that William did not love me, and had no intention of honouring the unofficial engagement between us. I was only surprised that the storm did not break the very next day.

Convinced that he had sped to the Parsonage with a proposal on his lips, seizing the opportunity of finding Miss Bennet alone (indisposed or otherwise), I entered the breakfast room on the following morning in a fine state of trepidation. Mama and Edward were already there, discussing William's extraordinary behaviour; he had returned to Rosings shortly after the Collinses' departure, and retired to his room without any explanation as to where he had been.

When he finally joined us for breakfast he looked tired and agitated, and cut short our expressions of concern with one statement: "I beg your pardon, ma'am. Forgive me, cousin – I am not disposed for conversation. I did not sleep well." He ate a few mouthfuls, excused himself, and went out again; we did not see him for the rest of the day.

He returned in time for dinner, seemingly in a calmer frame of mind but still tight lipped and pale, as though keeping his composure with difficulty. I concluded that he was putting off the moment of revelation. For the first time in my life, I was tempted to despise him. If he loved Miss Bennet, he must brave his family's displeasure; there was nothing else for it. To be sure, this was just such an unequal match as he had advised his friend Bingley against making, and would expose him to censure in some quarters, but when all was said and done she was a gentleman's daughter and there would be no impropriety in their union. He must surely do right by Mama, and by me, and declare himself before he and Edward left Rosings on the following day.

But leave without explanation he did, and I could only presume that Miss Bennet had persuaded him to secrecy. Perhaps she had insisted he speak first to her father - that would at least be honourable, though I doubted Mama would see it in that light.

They called briefly at the Parsonage before their departure, and Edward expressed disappointment at not having found Miss Elizabeth at home; he had waited, he said, some time in hopes of her return, while William walked back to Rosings. I wondered briefly whether she might already have left for Hertfordshire, but recollected that Mr Collins would never allow his guests to depart without paying their respects to Mama. *He* could surely not be party to the secret, though his wife might well be in her friend's confidence; I would be watching Mrs Collins like a hawk.

William said his goodbyes in a distracted state; his demeanour did not go unnoticed by Mama, who put it down to his 'peculiar attachment to Rosings'. She declared her intention of visiting Georgiana in London, and hinted that I might accompany her – would William be in town next month? He replied shortly that he did not know. He would not even look me in the eye as he took my hand and mumbled his farewell.

I bid a much more affectionate goodbye to Edward, in whom I longed to confide – but he clearly had no suspicions of his own, and it was hardly the best time to burden him with mine. I made him promise to visit again as soon as his military duties allowed.

Mama found herself so dull at the loss of her nephews that when Mr Collins made his call on the following day she sent him back with an invitation to his party to dine with us that evening. I was horrified at the prospect, and considered feigning a headache myself; but the thought that Mama might publicly attribute my indisposition to William's departure made me determine to see the evening out. The conflict of emotions with which I greeted Miss Elizabeth may well be imagined; and she, though tolerably composed, had not half so much to say for herself as usual. Was this, I wondered, the silence of rapture?

Mama, of course, had other ideas. "You seem out of spirits, Miss Bennet!" she observed. "You are thinking, perhaps, of your return to Hertfordshire. I am out of spirits myself, as is Anne; I am particularly fond of my nephews, and they were sorry to leave us. Poor Darcy seemed to feel it most acutely; his attachment to Rosings certainly increases!"

I looked towards Miss Bennet and found her gaze already upon me; I turned hastily away to smile weakly at Mr Collins, who was bowing in my direction.

"Miss Bennet, Miss Lucas, you must put off your departure!" declared Mama with sudden animation. "If you remain here for another month - I am sure your families can spare you - it will be in my power to take you as far as London in the barouche, for I shall be visiting my niece Georgiana in June. What say you to that?"

Once again, I was horrified; but Miss Bennet, to my great relief, insisted they must leave as planned.

An uncle was expecting them in London, in transpired, and they were to travel back to Hertfordshire from his house; the arrangements were already in place, her father had written only last week to hurry her return. (Strangely, this caused me my greatest pang of jealousy so far – she had a father who loved and missed her.)

By the time the Collinses' guests left Hunsford, I could not wait to be rid of them. Mama had summoned them to Rosings on at least three more occasions to inquire into the particulars of their journey home, the circumstances of the uncle in London, and the progress of their packing; and when they called to say their last goodbyes she graciously invited them to visit the Parsonage again next year. I wondered how Miss Bennet kept her countenance, knowing as she must do that if and when she came again to Rosings, it would not be as the guest of Mr Collins!

As I made my courtesy she met my troubled gaze with a fleeting expression of pity; what had William been saying to her about me? I was briefly tempted to take her hand, give some sign that I knew her secret, impress her with my powers of perception and lofty detachment – but it was too late. As the carriage wheels gathered speed upon the gravel I willed her away as fast and as far as possible.

*****chapter twenty*****

The remaining weeks of May passed slowly indeed. Apart from the Collinses we had no visitors, and I was left to let speculation feed upon imagination uninterrupted by the demands of the outside world. It was not a healthy pastime. It was one thing, I found, to accept that any feelings William might once have had for me were dead, and quite another to know that they had been revived by someone else! I had not until now had any real occasion for jealousy; but now that I knew – or rather, *believed,* for I had as yet no actual proof – that he was in love with Elizabeth Bennet, my imagination leapt from the arms of resignation into the fiery bosom of unmitigated rivalry. I pictured them walking arm in arm, William drawing her close beside him, leaning tenderly towards her with his dark and eager gaze, brushing her cheek with his fingers, his lips; my imagination took me further, each step more painful than the last. It was shameful, but I could not stop myself. All this, I told myself, was happening now to Elizabeth Bennet and not to me, and there was nothing in the world I could do about it. Or was there? I toyed with the idea of imparting my suspicions to Mama; without proof she would surely refuse to believe me, but she might be worried enough to make inquiries. She would make them however in such a way as to involve all concerned in mortification of the acutest kind, and it was still just possible that I might be mistaken - how would I ever live down such humiliation? No, there was nothing for it but to suffer in silence; to suspect all, to say nothing, and to be prepared for the worst.

I tried desperately to to occupy my mind with other matters; I became impatient to visit Georgiana in London, daunted though I was by the prospect of the journey. However when a letter came from William confirming that he was to remain at Pemberley until late July, Mama could no longer see any reason for me to accompany her.

"You would not be equal to it, Anne," she declared; "Not in this heat – do you think I have not noticed how pale and fatigued you are lately? Look at you, you are all a-tremble, starting at the smallest noise – you could no more bear the journey to London than a sea-voyage to the Indies!"

Of course I was trembling, for she held his letter in her hand and had as yet given it only a hasty perusal. When she finished reading, however, she put down her lorgnette with perfect equanimity.

"He will not be there, Anne," she persisted gently; "he has much to attend to at Pemberley. He asks kindly to be remembered to you. I know you must wish to see Georgiana, but it is my intention to persuade her to come here for few days before returning to Derbyshire for the summer. This Mrs Annesley is by all accounts a sensible sort of person, and if I find her to my liking I shall invite her also, that they may travel down together. Now is not that a preferable scheme to your having to endure the journey to London, and the company of those Bingleys who seem constantly to be foisting themselves upon my niece? I read here that Miss Bingley and the married sister, Mrs Hurst, are become very intimate with her – those are his exact words, *'they are become very intimate with my sister'.* The Bingley fortune was all acquired from trade, you know; I am not in the least sanguine about the association, for all my nephew speaks highly of his friend."

As relief and disappointment mingled in my breast, I managed to assimilate two important facts. Firstly, William's letter contained no revelation of his engagement to Miss Bennet, and no reference to his going into Hertfordshire; this must surely mean that they were not yet engaged, for he could not have put off the announcement any longer if they were. I had been precipitous then in imagining a clandestine proposal, though I could not believe myself mistaken about his feelings. Secondly, my mother now had an ulterior reason for inviting herself to London, viz. the Bingleys, concerning whom she had obviously formed the very same suspicions that I had lately been harbouring myself. In London she could meet them, and decide for herself whether Mr Charles Bingley would make a suitable husband for Miss Georgiana Darcy should the occasion arise. I laughed inwardly at the thought of her objecting to a fortune acquired from trade, when we were in much more present danger of connecting to a family with no fortune whatsoever; but of course I said nothing, and when the time came I waved her off as cheerfully as I could. Whilst awaiting her return I passed the time with rides in the Park, and spillage with Mrs Jenkinson.

She was back within the week, and the breathless manner of her arrival and her greeting – "Oh! Anne, I must speak with you alone; I have something so shocking to tell as you will not believe!" - caused my heart to lurch within me as I followed her into the morning room. So the news is out, I told myself, resolving that nothing she was about to say should discompose me. She seated herself by the window, dismissed Wilson and Dawkins with an impatient wave of the hand, and then proceeded to relate a circumstance that was so far from what I had been expecting that I had trouble, initially, in comprehending the import of it.

Georgiana, said Mama, had received her most kindly. She had found her much grown, with a fine womanly figure, and in good health though perhaps lacking a little of her former *joie de vivre*. Her chaperone Mrs Annesley was a mature and sensible person, with the manners of a gentlewoman; she was forced to admit that her nephews had made an excellent second choice. She had made the acquaintance of the Bingleys, as anticipated: Charles Bingley seemed 'a pleasant enough young man, though a little insipid, and weak-jawed which was always a bad sign; but on the whole, she could find no fault with his manners.' The sisters, however, were 'every bit as ill-bred as one expects from new money' and the brother-in-law, Mr Hurst, was 'an odious man, a stranger to good manners and clearly the worse for drink.' She had observed Georgiana closely in Mr Bingley's company, and was 'satisfied that her behaviour gave no reason to suspect an attachment on her part; she was not so sure about him, however, as he seemed excessively anxious to please.'

She had been in London just three days when William arrived unexpectedly, apparently most anxious to speak with her. (Here I steeled myself, studied the lace cuff on my sleeve, and avoided my mother's eye.)

Once they were alone, she continued, he begged pardon for his directness but asked if there were any ulterior motive for her visit. Mama was surprised, but saw no reason to dissemble; she told him that she came to see how her niece got on, to persuade her to visit Rosings before travelling North, and to see for herself what company she was keeping in London.

And how did she find Georgiana? William asked. Mama replied that she had grown into an accomplished young woman, but seemed a little guarded in her manner, less vivacious than her former self. And what did she think of her friends, the Bingleys? Charles Bingley seemed pleasant enough, but she did not care for the sisters. To speak plainly, they were not a family to which she would wish to be connected.

William then said he had suspected her to be harbouring some illusion such as this, and had come down on purpose to assure her that no attachment existed, or was likely to exist, between Georgiana and Charles Bingley. He desired her to take his word on this, and not to question Georgiana on the matter – the subject might cause her distress, and he would now explain the reason why.

Last summer Georgiana *had* visited Ramsgate with Mrs Younge, and it had been William's intention to join them towards the end of their stay. Finding himself able to make the journey into Kent somewhat earlier than expected he had come down unannounced, anticipating a joyous welcome. To his considerable perturbation, the first person he saw upon arriving in Ramsgate was George Wickham, deep in conversation with the a coachman at the Eagle Inn. A chill of foreboding clutched at his breast; he followed him, at a distance and unobserved, to find where he was headed. His feelings upon seeing him enter the house where his sister and Mrs Younge were lodged may well be imagined! He burst in upon them, and Georgiana's confusion told him all that he needed to know. Once Wickham had been sent packing, it took very little time to get the full story from her.

George Wickham had apparently been a frequent visitor to Mrs Younge's London address, all unbeknownst to Edward and William, since he had asked Georgiana to say nothing of it in her letters home. She had believed his assurance that her brother's ill feeling was based upon a misunderstanding, and been persuaded to admit his company, and later his declarations of love, with pleasure. His manners, always charming, were enough to recommend him to a woman of Mrs Younge's weak understanding; and in short, an elopement had been planned with her full connivance, and would have been carried out within a couple of days!

"You may imagine, ma'am," said William to Mama, "how I felt, and how I acted. Wickham left Ramsgate immediately, and I took it upon myself to remove Georgiana from Mrs Younge's care with equal haste. I know this distressed you, but ignorant as you were of the facts I could not bring myself to lay before you a circumstance that would only distress you still further. Concern for my sister's good name, as well as for her feelings, has prevented me from acquainting anyone other than Colonel Fitzwilliam with these events and it is this same consideration that leads me to tell you of it now. I beg of you, ma'am, say nothing to her of this interview. It has taken her all this time to recover her equanimity, and to feel herself equal even to the society of her friends. The Bingleys of course know nothing; but it pleases me to see her at ease in their company, and I would not have her happiness disturbed by questioning about attachments, engagements of anything of the sort. I will tell my sister at some point that I have acquainted you with the facts, and I hope she may be assured of your full forgiveness and understanding, as she is of mine. Let us only be grateful that our family has been spared so great a humiliation, and that Georgiana is safe and well."

What a succession of emotions swept over me as Mama related this story! I was shocked, certainly; shocked at George Wickham, whom I knew to be less than respectable but had not thought capable of such downright wickedness; shocked, it must be admitted, that Georgiana had allowed his attentions; and shocked beyond anything, mortified, that my erstwhile governess and friend Mrs Younge should have countenanced and encouraged such a thing. I racked my memory for some hint, some allusion in her letters or in Georgiana's, that Wickham had become more than a childhood friend – should I have read between the lines, could I possibly have foreseen this? And what must William have thought of us, for having recommended Mrs Younge? No wonder, no wonder had had avoided us for so long. Perhaps he blamed *me*; at the very least he must consider me a wretched judge of character. And it was true, was it not, that I had known Mrs Younge to be giddy and foolish; but surely, no-one could have foreseen such a thing!

Mortification gave way to anger as I considered how easily, how wilfully, my former governess had imposed upon us all. Had she no gratitude, no loyalty at least to me? Had she not stopped to think what effect this elopement must have? Had she deliberately sought to drive a wedge between the Darcys and the de Bourghs, just because William had snubbed her? And to think I had forgiven all her faults, and considered her a friend!

And lastly, I must admit, I experienced pangs of jealousy – yes, even in such circumstances – that at just sixteen my cousin had, like one of Miss Burney's heroines, been embroiled in a romantic adventure! I was ashamed of the sentiment, and aware that had the elopement taken place I would have pitied her from the bottom of my heart – but jealousy still managed to surface in the midst of my agitation.

Mama expressed herself loudly and at length on the depravity of George Wickham.

"Ungrateful, abominable man! He has disgraced his father's memory and thrown my brother-in-law's generosity back in the face of his family. He had no real intention of studying the law, you know; he wasted all the money that my nephew advanced him in lieu of his taking orders, and then had the effrontery to change his mind, and ask to be furnished with a living after all! And what do you think he is doing now? He has gone into the Army! Darcy actually encountered him in Hertfordshire; he has taken a commission with the Militia recently quartered at Meryton! Naturally, he refused to acknowledge him. He wishes never to have to speak his name again. No more do I, I assure you. Of course it was my niece's fortune he was after – that, and the destruction of the family that nursed him as a viper in the bosom!"

The subject of vipers in the family bosom led her naturally to Mrs Younge, whom she declared to be a scheming hussy, a consummate actress who had duped us all.

"I wonder at you, Anne, for keeping up a correspondence with her for so long," she said, conveniently forgetting that our last exchange of letters had been at her own express request. "Had *I* been her correspondent, I would certainly have been able to decipher what she was about. But you are too trusting; when to comes to character, you take all for granted. You lack insight, my dear."

The injustice of this accusation goaded me to inquire whether William had made any mention of Miss Elizabeth Bennet; she looked at me as though I were utterly mad.

"Of course not, child. What on earth has Miss Bennet to do with anything?"

I shrugged, and said nothing, and listened dutifully as she continued to rail against Mrs Younge, George Wickham, and ungrateful servants in general. Hindsight rather than insight, I reflected, was my mother's indubitable forte.

*****chapter twenty-one*****

It transpired that the revelation of Georgiana's escapade had caused Mama to think twice about inviting her to Rosings; whether because she needed time to absorb the information, or because she could not trust herself to keep her knowledge of it a secret, she did not divulge. Instead, she had made a promise on my behalf that I would write to my cousin at Pemberley over the summer. I agreed to this somewhat reluctantly, since I doubted whether our old, easy intimacy could be re-established following all the events of the past year. Nevertheless I composed a cheerful letter, making no mention of Ramsgate and concentrating instead upon the continued eccentricities of Mr Collins, the forbearance of his wife and the brief introduction to our circle of Sir William Lucas, Miss Maria Lucas, and Miss Elizabeth Bennet. I mentioned that I knew them to be acquainted with the Bingleys, and wondered whether either they or William had spoken of them?

I had to wait nearly three weeks for a reply; but the letter when it came contained rather more information than I was expecting.

Georgiana began with apologies for the delay. The Bingleys and the Hursts had been staying at Pemberley, and the business of entertaining them had kept both herself and William busy; and as chance would have it, they had lately been joined by the very Miss Bennet of whom I had written - Miss Elizabeth, who was holidaying in Derbyshire with her aunt and uncle! The aunt, Mrs Gardiner, had spent her girlhood at Lambton and had persuaded them to come and view the house; they had thought the family from home, and had been most surprised to encounter William as they strolled by the lake. This 'happy co-incidence', as Georgiana described it, had resulted in an invitation to dinner, and the introduction of Miss Bennet and the Gardiners to the Pemberley household.

I smiled to myself at the ease with which William had convinced his sister that Elizabeth Bennet's arrival in Derbyshire was accidental; for myself, I believed no such thing, though I knew not whether his invitation or her importunity lay behind it. At any rate, she seemed to have made a favourable impression:

'I liked her very much,' wrote Georgiana; *'we all did, excepting Miss Bingley, but then she is always so critical. She quite angered William by commenting unfavourably on Miss Bennet's appearance; he rushed to her defence and declared her to be one of the handsomest women of his acquaintance! Caroline was sorely put out. Miss Bennet is, as you say, of a lively temperament, and I found her pleasant company; her relatives, the Gardiners, are likewise most agreeable. We were hoping to see*

more of them, but yesterday they were called unexpectedly back to Hertfordshire; it seems one of the family has been taken ill. I hope it is not too serious, and that we shall have the pleasure of seeing them again at some point.

'*William is also to leave us tomorrow; he has urgent business in town, and I wish he had not sprung it upon me in this manner, for I am now left to entertain our guests alone. Mrs Annesley assures me that I will be the perfect hostess, but I shrink from the responsibility – like you, I find long evenings in company exhausting, and I have not your excuse of delicate health so must do as best I can. I hope that William will not be away for long; he sends you his warm regards and asks to be remembered to my Aunt, as do I; it was most pleasant to see her in town last month.*

'*I remain, my dear Cousin,*
'*Your affectionate friend,*
'*Georgiana Darcy.*'

I laid down the letter with a shaking hand, glad that Mama was not hovering at my elbow expecting to be acquainted with its contents. Although I had now been waiting over two months to hear news of Miss Bennet and William, I had not expected it from such a quarter, and with so evident an endorsement of approval. I reminded myself that Georgiana was in all probability only dimly aware of our mothers' plans concerning William and myself, but all the same I would have expected her to express some surprise - she had obviously noted her brother's admiration for Miss Bennet, and must speculate as to where it might lead. But perhaps he could do no wrong in her eyes. Her trust in him was absolute, and suspicion, as the events of last year had shown, was not in her nature. I secreted the letter in my bureau and made no mention of it to Mama; her comments and questions would only distress me, and the next communication we received from the Darcys would undoubtedly reveal all.

It soon transpired, however, that the matters were not to be that straightforward.

"And how are your family in Hertfordshire, Mrs Collins?" inquired Mama when they next came to drink tea with us; "I trust that your parents are both well?"

"Perfectly so, I thank you, ma'am," replied Mrs Collins, somewhat cautiously I thought.

"A letter arrived from Sir William just this morning," volunteered her husband when she failed to elaborate further, "containing news of a most distressing nature."

"Indeed?" Mama leaned forward, her curiosity aroused; Mrs Collins looked vexed, and made a cautionary gesture, which her husband assiduously ignored.

"The letter was addressed to my wife, of course, but the news concerns a relative of mine – Miss Lydia Bennet, my cousin's youngest daughter. It is a very distressing circumstance indeed, and I am heartily sorry for her parents, the more so as the fault must lie partly with them. Your Ladyship's perspicacity in commenting to my cousin Elizabeth upon the imprudence of allowing five unmarried daughters to be out in society at once could not have been more prescient! Now the whole world may see what has come of it!"

"Well, and what *has* come of it, Mr Collins?" urged Mama with ill-disguised impatience.

"She is gone, eloped – worse than eloped, for no marriage is known to have taken place – with an officer in the Militia that was quartered at Meryton last autumn!"

"Good heavens!" ejaculated Mama, amazed, as was I, to be hearing of yet another elopement hot upon the heels of Georgiana's escapade. "When did this happen? Has she been gone from Hertfordshire long?"

"They left from Brighton ma'am, over a week ago; the Militia is presently quartered there and my cousin Lydia had been staying with the Colonel, as the guest of his wife. Heaven knows what her parents were thinking of in allowing a girl of sixteen to accept such an invitation! It was thought they were headed for Gretna Green, but they have only been traced as far as London, and are now presumed to be concealed somewhere in the metropolis. Her father and uncle are conducting a search for them there – is that no so, my dear?"

He turned to his wife for verification, and she nodded silently. I felt for her, knowing her to be a close friend of the Bennet family; but the greater part of my mind was calculating what effect all this must have upon William, for of course *this* was the reason for Miss Elizabeth's hasty departure with the Gardiners from Pemberley, and if not already privy to the details he could not remain in ignorance for long. News of an elopement is not easily hushed up, as we would all have found to our cost had the Ramsgate episode not been circumvented...

Mama was now probing the Collinses about Lydia Bennet's character; even Mrs Collins admitted her to be a silly, headstrong girl, indulged and unchecked by a doting mother, and her husband opined that her disposition must be 'naturally wicked'. Mama reflected with pleasure that Mrs Bennet was now reaping the whirlwind, having neglected her maternal duties; and it was only after these musings had run their course that she thought to inquire what was the name of the officer?

"For it is he," said she, "who must bear the best part of the blame, whatever the girl's shortcomings; and I hope most heartily that he will either be forced to marry her, or take his share in her ruin."

"He is someone whom I believe to be known to your nephew, Lady Catherine," replied Mr Collins, evidently not sorry to be shifting the attention from his family onto ours; "At least, that is what I have heard, though I am nor sure in what capacity -"

"My nephew? You allude, I presume, to Colonel Fitzwilliam?"

"To Mr Darcy, ma'am. Mr Wickham, I believe, is

formerly from Derbyshire, and was there acquainted with Mr Darcy."

My mother is not often rendered speechless; but the exclamation, "Wickham! Good God, can this be possible?" broke not from her lips but from mine, as we stared at one another aghast.

Mr Collins was eager to assure us that George Wickham was indeed the man. "Sir William writes that the whole of Meryton is shocked, for he had made himself very popular while he was there and nobody suspected him capable of such a thing; but it has since emerged that he left behind debts, substantial gaming debts, and tradesmen's debts in addition. And I do recall hearing, Lady Catherine, that Mr Darcy would not admit his company. He was thought overly proud on account of it I believe, but now his discrimination is more than justified."

"Yes, indeed!" cried Mama, recovering her voice; "my nephew knows George Wickham's character well, and would have advised any gentleman against allowing his daughters such company had he been consulted on the matter. And to think that he was to have been a clergyman! Yes, you may well look shocked, Mr Collins – he is the son of the late Mr Darcy's steward, educated at my brother's expense, and intended for the Church! That such generosity should have been wasted on such an object!"

She lapsed once more into silence, musing no doubt, as I was musing myself, on the narrowness by which our own Georgiana had escaped the same fate as Lydia Bennet.

She roused herself when the Collinses took their leave, to remark with ill-disguised satisfaction that she was heartily sorry not only for Mr and Mrs Bennet, "but also for your friend Miss Elizabeth, whom we had the pleasure of meeting in the Spring; for surely this dreadful circumstance must affect her chances of making a good marriage herself. Who will now wish to connect themselves with such a family?"

Who indeed, I echoed silently, as it slowly dawned upon me that this could change everything; *who in particular* will hardly now be able to make an alliance that must connect him to his sister's would-be seducer? No wonder William had quitted Pemberley so suddenly; very likely Miss Elizabeth had told him the real reason for her departure, and he had found himself unable to continue playing the genial host. What must he be feeling, I wondered, and how will he act? His disappointment must be severe. Is he thanking the heavens that he delayed his proposal, or cursing himself for a fatal hesitation? Would family pride or unrequited love prove the stronger emotion?

It was only with difficulty that I dissuaded Mama from writing to William at once, to acquaint him with what he must already know.

"He will hear of it soon enough, Mama," I said, "and think how it must distress him; for he could have prevented it, could he not, if he had made George Wickham's character known to the world."

"And expose his own family to ridicule in the

process? I am heartily glad he did no such thing. As regards my niece, we had all better follow his example and remain silent. Let us hope that Wickham will marry the Bennet girl, and there will be an end of it."

"She has nothing that can tempt him to marry her, Mama; unlike Georgiana, she has no fortune. He will ruin her, and proceed on his way unpunished, perhaps to ruin others. William must speak out, I think, if this proves to be the case."

"I will think him a fool if he does, Anne. What are these Bennets to us, after all?"

I shook my head sadly, and said nothing.

I would dearly have liked to write again to Georgiana, who I knew must suffer greatly when the news came out – though it would at least remove any lingering affection she might harbour for George Wickham! But I could not express my sympathy without betraying my knowledge of her story, which would only increase her mortification. So I wrote instead to Edward, whose regiment I knew to be quartered for the summer in Kent; and deprived as I was of a confidante (for Mama had forbidden me to acquaint Mrs Jenkinson with the particulars regarding Georgiana), I poured out my heart to him. I told him of my knowledge of the Ramsgate debacle, of Wickham's elopement with Lydia Bennet, and also of my long-held suspicions concerning William and Elizabeth Bennet. I knew that he would not betray my confidence.

Whilst I awaited his reply, we learned from Mr

Collins that the fugitive lovers had finally been discovered, and that following some swift financial negotiations a belated marriage had taken place. Mama declared herself greatly relieved.

"So, Lydia Bennet is saved!" she cried, "if salvation it can be called, to become the wife of such a man. I suppose Mr Bennet has been obliged to lay out a large sum of money to bring it about? For you say there were debts to be discharged, and a man of Wickham's character is not to be prevailed upon by appeals to his honour alone. Do you know where they were discovered, and by whom?"

"I do not, your Ladyship; I know none of the particulars," replied Mr Collins with evident regret; "but my cousin is a gentleman of limited means, and I cannot imagine a large sum to have been within his power. My wife believes the family to be indebted to the brother-in-law, Mr Gardiner, for his help in the matter."

"Ah, that is the uncle in London - a solicitor, I believe. He must be doing well for himself, to be able to assist his niece in such a way! I hope she is duly grateful. Did the marriage then take place from Mr Gardiner's house?"

"I believe so, Your Ladyship."

"And where will they live, do you suppose? Surely not in the neighbourhood of Meryton?"

"No indeed, ma'am. Mr Wickham has resigned his present commission, and taken up another with the Regulars, who are stationed in the North Country. He and his wife will travel there as soon as they leave

Longbourn."

"Longbourn! They have been received at the house, then? Mr Bennet must be a most accommodating father-in-law!"

"A good deal *too* accommodating in my opinion, Your Ladyship!" cried Mr Collins with some vehemence; "To receive such a couple into his house seems almost an endorsement of their sin; had *I* been consulted on the matter I would have advised most strenuously against it. My cousin is a Christian gentleman, and as such must show his daughter forgiveness – but to allow her back under his roof is surely taking things too far. Had *I* the misfortune to have so wicked a child, I would not allow her name or her husband's to be mentioned in my hearing!"

Mama, somewhat taken aback by so parsimonious a notion of Christian forgiveness, merely commented that at least a marriage had taken place, even if it were a patched-up affair, and that for this we must all be grateful. She then turned the conversation to Mrs Collins' interesting state of health, which had prevented her from accompanying her husband to Rosings on this occasion and concerning which she had much to advise and recommend.

*****chapter twenty-two*****

When Mrs Jenkinson and I returned from our afternoon drive a few days later, we saw an unknown horse being led to the stables; evidence of a visitor's arrival.

"Who can it be, alone and on horseback?" I wondered aloud; and Mrs Jenkinson's speculating that 'it might be Mr Darcy' caused me to step down from the phaeton with some trepidation. It was with pleasure, however, that I learned from the groom that 'Colonel Fitzwilliam is just arrived, and has gone into the house.'

I found him sitting with Mama in the drawing-room; he rose as I entered, with a cheerful greeting. He had the presence of mind not to mention my letter, and explained his unscheduled visit by the proximity of his summer quarters.

"I could not be in Kent without calling upon you both; I came only to inquire after your health, Anne, and of course to pay my respects to you, ma'am. As I was saying, I will not extend my stay beyond a couple of days."

Such thoughtfulness earned him an invitation to stay as long as he liked, and when Mama had completed her inquiries concerning the health of his father and his brother's ever-increasing family, she bustled away to advise Mrs Henderson of the addition of a guest to the household, leaving us to converse alone.

Drawing his chair close to mine, Edward immediately produced my letter and began to chide me for not having confided in him sooner.

"Had I known your suspicions, Anne, I could have found a way of inquiring into the matter at an earlier stage; but unfortunately events have overtaken us. I have spoken with our cousin; I met him briefly in London. I confined my inquiries to the business with Wickham and the youngest Miss Bennet, and excused my interference by concern for our ward. I do not know what to make of it, Anne – he made no mention of Miss Elizabeth, and the facts *would* bear a different interpretation – he could be acting in deference to his sister's feelings – I would not have you agitate yourself unnecessarily..."

Such a Collins-like preamble was hardly designed to prevent agitation, and I begged him to explain himself without further delay. Edward sighed, and passed a hand across his brow.

"Well then, to be brief," he said, "It was our cousin who discovered the guilty couple in London - they were lodging, as he suspected they might be, with our old friend Mrs Younge. It was he who returned the girl to her uncle, he who laid down a substantial sum to persuade Wickham to marry her, and he who escorted the bridegroom to the wedding. And finally, he has charged Mr and Mrs Gardiner to say nothing of his involvement, but to take all the credit for themselves! When I asked him *why* he had gone to all this trouble and expense, he replied that he saw it as reparation for damage caused; had he not been so determined to conceal our family's experience of Wickham's profligacy, he said, the man's character would have been widely known. Neither Mr Bennet nor Colonel Forster would have allowed him Miss Lydia's company, and the elopement would never have taken place. He spoke so earnestly that I did not feel able to questions his motives by mentioning Miss Elizabeth; and I still think, cousin, that it is one thing to be of assistance to a deserving family and quite another to wish to become a member of it, especially as it must now include George Wickham. But it remains an extraordinary act of generosity, however one looks at it; and our cousin intends to accompany Charles Bingley into Hertfordshire when he returns there, as I believe he may already have done."

I nodded silently, and reached for his hand, which he gave me with ready affection saying, "Anne, I hardly know what to say. I am aware of my aunt's wishes concerning yourself and our cousin, and have always assumed them to be your wishes also; but as for *his* wishes, I am entirely in the dark; he has never mentioned the matter in my hearing." He hesitated briefly before continuing, "*Are* they your wishes, Anne? Or merely my aunt's?"

Here we were interrupted by the entrance of Wilson bearing a tray of refreshment, and he hastily withdrew his hand. I speculated ruefully that were it anyone but Edward, this gesture could lend a particular import to his question; but he poured us each a glass of wine and resumed his seat without the slightest embarrassment, and only brotherly concern shone from his eyes as he watched me circle a finger round the rim of my glass, trying to compose an answer.

"I hardly know," I said at last, "*what* my wishes are; I seem never to have had the luxury of choice. I was ten years old when I first discovered that I was expected to marry William; Papa told me that it would be a happy arrangement for the family, but that I should not be forced to it if my feelings were opposed when the time came. Since then I seem to have spent my entire life trying to decide what my feelings for William are! I did fancy myself in love with him at one stage – before Papa died, before I fell ill – and allowed myself to fancy that he felt the same. But when he came to visit me afterwards, any admiration he might have been harbouring for me evaporated on the spot – I saw it in his face, in his manner. And you know what the sonnet says – we used to read it together, did we not - *'Love is not love, that alters when it alteration finds'.* Since then he has behaved so – you know how he behaves towards me, Edward, you have seen it for yourself. He does not love me, and with so little encouragement I cannot allow myself to - I would like to be married and loved one day, but -"

"I am sure, dearest Anne, that you will be both, let Darcy choose as he may!" interrupted Edward, placing down his glass and leaning forward to take my hand once again. "I am relieved to hear you say that you are not in love with him. If what you suspect proves true, you will be able to bear the insult with no lasting hurt to your feelings. And in time, you will look around you and realise that our cousin is not the only personable man in the world! As the last of the de Bourghs, you will certainly have no shortage of suitors once you are known to be eligible!"

I laughed nervously, shuddering inwardly at the thought, and turned the conversation back to William.

"Do you remember how he rebuked you for paying too much attention to Miss Bennet? *'It would be unfortunate indeed if she had formed any expectations'* - were not those his word? We all thought it most unjust. But if he were thinking of himself all the time..."

"Then his interference would make sense, it is true. But what of his attitude to Bingley's attachment, and his interference there? He led me to believe that the lady's unsuitability lay not in any fault of character, but solely in her inferior connections. Would he be so nice on behalf of his friend, and not as regards himself? It seems illogical."

"People in love seldom *are* logical," I said seriously; "I have read all about it in Miss Burney's novels."

Edward laughed long and loudly at this, and I could not help but join him; Mama, entering the room to find us thus diverted, looked exceedingly suspicious and inspected the contents of the decanter.

Edward agreed to remain with us 'til the end of the week. Mama lost no time in recounting the story of Wickham's elopement and marriage, and was most put out to find that he had already heard the news from William.

"Oh! So Darcy knows of it, does he? Then why did he not write to me, instead of leaving me to hear it from Mr Collins? He knows how concerned I am for dear Georgiana; did she never reply to your letter, Anne? I must write to Pemberley, and invite them both to Rosings for the occasion of Anne's birthday; you will join us Fitzwilliam, will you not?"

A brief glance passed between Edward and myself as he replied calmly, "With the greatest pleasure, ma'am; but Darcy, I believe, has gone into Hertfordshire, and stays at Netherfield Hall with his friend Charles Bingley."

Mama was now doubly astonished. "Hertfordshire? He goes into Hertfordshire so soon after Wickham has been there? I wonder he can bear to be near the place. Has he no consideration for his sister's feelings? I am astonished to hear this, Fitzwilliam; I am exceedingly displeased. I shall write to my niece – no, Anne shall write – she stays at Pemberley, does she not, Fitzwilliam?"

Edward nodded an assent.

"Then you shall write to her again, Anne, and say that she and Mrs Annesly will be most welcome to spend a few days at Rosings before returning to town. At least the Bingleys are out of the way, if they are all at Netherfield. That is one thing to be grateful for."

This time I had no reluctance in complying with her wishes, and was pleased to be able to mention the Bennet sisters without resorting to subterfuge, since the Wickham marriage was now obviously common knowledge. I was not sure, however, whether William would have confided his own involvement in the matter, so I merely asked whether either of them had heard from Elizabeth Bennet following her sister's marriage, commenting that the outcome must be a great relief to the family - *'for when you last wrote to me Miss Bennet and the Gardiners had just left Pemberley in haste, and it must have been news of her sister's elopement that occasioned this sudden departure. I do hope that she is well, and that none of the Miss Bennets will suffer too great a loss of consequence on account of their sister's unwise conduct.'*

That ought to do it, I thought to myself; I have betrayed no knowledge of Georgiana's own adventure with George Wickham, and if she has anything to tell me regarding her brother and Miss Bennet I have given her an opening.

I concluded with my mother's invitation to Rosings, wondering guiltily as I sealed the letter what my poor cousin would make of such a double-edged piece of correspondence. She must surely conclude that she was being summoned to be interrogated about her brother's intentions; I imagined her hastily dispatching a plea for help to Hertfordshire.

Ah well, I reflected as I dusted the seal, we will be reaping the whirlwind soon enough. Much as I dreaded Mama's reaction, I could not suppress a frisson of excitement; I was Pandora, with my hand upon the lid of that fateful box.

*****chapter twenty-three*****

Georgiana's reply was very prompt, arriving on the day after Edward's departure. How I missed his support as I mounted the stairs to my old schoolroom, where I knew I should have privacy to peruse the letter uninterrupted! I broke the seal with a trembling hand and devoured the contents in haste; then re-read the whole of it slowly and carefully. Once again, I had thought there could be no surprises left, only to be confronted by a new and unexpected turn of events. It made sense, however; it made perfect sense, that his sentiments would have undergone so material a change in the light of his present position.

As I slowly descended the stairs, I heard the unmistakeable tones of Mr Collins and the gentle interspersions of his wife emanating from the drawing room. I entered to hear my mother exclaiming that she would not have thought it possible, that Charles Bingley must surely have taken leave of his senses!

"What has Sir William Lucas to say on the matter? Surely the whole neighbourhood must be very much shocked and surprised?"

"On the contrary, your Ladyship, it was largely expected to have been announced last autumn; Mrs Bennet mentioned it to me herself when I was first at

Longbourn, and my wife informs me that Mr Bingley's quitting Netherfield last year caused greater surprise than the announcement of his engagement does now."

Mr Collins rose as he made this speech, to acknowledge my entrance; as I seated myself Mama explained,

"We are speaking, Anne, of Mr Bingley and the eldest Bennet girl – he is engaged to Jane Bennet! Can you believe such a thing possible? He thinks nothing of the scandal of her sister's elopement, seems to find it no shame to make such an inferior connection – I beg your pardon, Mr Collins, but I must speak as I find – I have no particularly high opinion of the Bingleys, but this is ridiculous! And Darcy is with him! He must be mortified by his friend's behaviour. Did you know, Mr Collins, that my nephew has been at Netherfield this past fortnight?"

"I did, your Ladyship, and according to my father-in-law -"

"I would not be surprised if he were to drop the acquaintance altogether now," continued Mama with satisfaction, oblivious to the confusion that suffused Mrs Collins' countenance at the mention of William's name. I observed it, however, and was able to interject calmly, indicating the letter in my hand, "I do not think that is very likely, Mama; I have here a letter from Georgiana, in which she says that William accompanied Mr Bingley into Hertfordshire in full knowledge of his intentions. Miss Bennet, you see, was the lady from whom he was so anxious to separate his friend last year! But now he has completely altered his opinion, and given the match his full approval."

"What, in spite of the connection with Wickham? Unthinkable!"

Mama's horror was evident, and a short silence ensued. It was broken by Mr Collins clearing his throat apologetically: "Far be it from me to contradict your Ladyship," he ventured, "but my father-in-law informs us that Mr Darcy as well as Mr Bingley has been seen to dine frequently at Longbourn."

"My nephew, dine at Longbourn! What possible occasion could there be for that?"

Mr Collins' courage failed him in the face of such indignation, and he bowed his head submissively. I wondered how much more he knew – he was a man of limited perception, but his wife was more astute, and very likely in Miss Elizabeth's confidence.

"Lady Catherine!" cried she, with well-staged urgency, "I beg your pardon, but I am not well. Would you be so kind as to allow me to retire to the sofa?"

There was no denying such a request from a woman in Mrs Collins' condition, and her husband supported her with great alacrity to the chaise longue while Mama rang for sal volatile and ordered the carriage to be ready when she had recovered herself. For a short while all was bustle and concern, and I pitied Mrs Collins exceedingly for it was plain to me that she must know all. She glanced swiftly and unhappily towards me as her husband and Mrs Jenkinson finally escorted her from the room; I smiled kindly upon her, and continued to smile as the doors closed behind them. Then I rose, crossed over to my mother's chair and placed Georgiana's letter in her lap.

'In response to your inquiry about the Bennet sisters,' she had written, *'I do have some news: our friend Mr Bingley is in love with the eldest sister, Jane! He has gone into Hertfordshire expressly to propose, and there seems little doubt that she will accept him, for an attachment was known to exist between them last autumn, though Caroline and Mrs Hurst always dismissed it as nothing. They were very much opposed to the idea, as was William, and I suspect it was their disapproval which prevented poor Mr Bingley from declaring himself earlier. Now of course they are doubly outraged, since the youngest Miss Bennet's marriage was thought to have put an end to any such possibility; but it seems to have had the opposite effect, and stirred their brother to new heights of courage and determination! For myself, I wish him well; and it seems that William is now of a like mind, which pleases me.*

'My brother has changed over this last year, Anne; I wonder whether you thought him changed, when he visited you in the Spring? And I think I know the cause; but before I say more, I must know your

opinion, for I would not distress you for the world. You have asked so many questions about Miss Elizabeth Bennet, that I wonder if you also suspect the possibility of an attachment between them? It seemed very evident during her brief stay here.

'I do hope, dear Cousin, that I have said nothing to cause you pain. Pray write again, and reassure me if you can. William is presently in London, but will be returning to Hertfordshire within the fortnight.

'Pray thank my Aunt for her kind invitation. Mrs Annesley and I would be very happy to visit Rosings, but I believe we must wait upon my brother's return from Hertfordshire before making any arrangements.

'I remain, dear Cousin,
'Your devoted friend, &c.'

When she finished reading, Mama laid down her lorgnette and remained silent for so long a time that I began to think she had fallen into a stupor, and that I might be able to leave the room unnoticed. As soon as I moved however, she sprang back to life and demanded angrily to know where I thought I was going?

"I am just going upstairs, Mama, to lie down for a while," I responded meekly, feeling sure that this must be a reasonable response to what had just been revealed.

"Not so fast, young lady," admonished Mama, waving Georgiana's letter before me; she then demanded to know what questions I had been asking about Miss Bennet, and why my cousin might possibly think that I suspected an attachment between that lady and my future husband.

It was the moment I had been dreading, but the words I had rehearsed so frequently did not fail me. Calmly and quietly I proceeded to enlighten her. I assured her that I had long ceased to think of William as my future husband, since he showed no sign of affection for me; that I had suspected an attachment between him and Miss Bennet since observing them together in the Spring; and that my suspicions had been confirmed by Georgiana's informing me that Miss Elizabeth Bennet had been received at Pemberley.

Mama shook her head vehemently throughout. "Nonsense!" she expostulated as soon as I had finished. "Tis all speculation, and gossip of the most pernicious kind. My nephew Darcy is engaged to *you,* Anne, and would never behave so dishonourably as to pay court to another woman under my very roof, or anywhere else. I refuse to believe it. He is engaged to *you.*"

I shook my head sadly. "I have reminded you many times, Mama, that no formal engagement exists between us. If William's inclination does not direct him towards me he is certainly not bound by honour. I am very much afraid, Mama, that this is no idle rumour – he is in love with Elizabeth Bennet."

"'We shall see about that!" declared Mama, ringing the bell for Wilson; when he entered she requested, with ominous calm, that a message be sent to Mr Collins expressing the hope that his wife was now feeling more comfortable, and requiring him to return to Rosings at his earliest convenience.

I was not privy to the interview that took place between Mama and Mr Collins that afternoon, but I watched from the landing as he left the drawing room twisting his hat in both hands in such a way as to crush it quite out of shape, and looking thoroughly crushed himself. I felt sorry for the poor man – the Bennets were his cousins, after all; and Mama, as she later explained to me, had laid upon him the task of confronting them, by letter, with her displeasure at the prospect of an alliance between her nephew and their daughter. I reflected that if Miss Elizabeth were a typical example of the Bennet temperament, this epistle would have little effect.

In the meantime Mama's outrage at having been deliberately deceived, as she saw it, by so many members of her family knew no bounds. Over breakfast the next morning, she repeatedly accused me of subterfuge, ingratitude and a spineless lack of self-interest. When her rant had run its course and she could find nothing further to say, she declared her intention of going into Hertfordshire herself to confront Miss Elizabeth at Longbourn, and extract from her a denial that any engagement existed between herself and William.

"Oh good Heavens, Mama, I beg you will do no such thing!" I implored; "Your arrival in Hertfordshire will rather be seen as a confirmation of it, can you not see that? There is surely no reason to expose yourself to such indignity. Go first to London if you must, and speak to William before he returns to Netherfield; if there is any denying to be done, it had better come from him."

But Mama would have none of my counsel. "Are you out of your senses, child? I would not dream of putting my nephew to such embarrassment! 'Tis quite possible he has no idea that such a rumour exists – and if he does, he must be mortified by the interpretation placed upon a little gallantry and exchange of pleasantries in a country neighbourhood! It will all be down to *her,* you mark my words. She has been spreading this report deliberately, aided and abetted by her sisters; these Bennets are a veritable nest of vipers! But she shall not be allowed to get away with it; I shall inform her that my nephew is engaged to *you,* and that any declaration she may have extracted from him in private is null and void."

I shook my head, appalled at the delusion that prompted so self-contradictory a speech and so reckless a plan. For the hundredth time, I repeated, "He is *not* engaged to me, Mama, and you cannot truthfully claim that he is. I have no particular liking for Miss Bennet, but look at it from her point of view: why should not William, as a single gentleman, make his own choice of wife? If *she* is that choice, why should she not accept him?"

"Because she is a young woman of inferior birth, of no importance in the world, and with no fortune whatsoever! Yes, she is a gentleman's daughter; but what of her mother? What of her uncles and aunts?

And merciful heavens, what of her brother-in-law, a steward's son, an infamous eloper? Such a connection would expose my nephew to the contempt of all who know him, and ruin him in the opinion of his dearest friends! Have you no consideration for your cousin's reputation and consequence?"

I shrugged resignedly. "Well, it looks as though they matter but little to him, so why should they matter to me?"

Mama regarded me through narrowed eyes, as though properly assessing me for the first time.

"So, you are happy to sit by and see your family's honour trodden into the mud. Have you no pride left for yourself, even if you have none for your cousin? Where will you find a husband when the de Bourghs become a laughing-stock? Have you thought of that? If your cousin will not marry you, who will?"

And with that question hanging unanswered in the air she quitted the room, calling loudly for Wilson to order the chaise, find Mrs Henderson, and send for Dawson immediately. I let her go without further protest; such a venomous farewell did not incline me to dissuade her from venting the remainder of her spleen upon Elizabeth Bennet.

*****chapter twenty-four*****

Mama was gone for two days, giving me ample opportunity to reflect upon her parting words and to imagine the lively interchange which her interview with Miss Bennet must certainly occasion. Miss Elizabeth knew her own interests too well to be submissive, of that I was convinced. I did occasionally allow myself to imagine my mother returning victorious, bearing the wounded and repentant William with her as a trophy; but in truth I did not think it even remotely probable.

I wondered what Papa would be saying to me now. He had reassured me all those years ago that I would not be forced into marriage, and had extended the same liberty to William. I decided that as long as he were satisfied that I did not feel myself wronged, he would champion his nephew's right to marry where he liked.

Then of course I had to face the question: *did* I feel myself wronged? It was the first thing Mrs Jenkinson asked me, gently pointing out the distinction between feeling wronged and feeling disappointed. I nodded slowly.

"Well, Mama will certainly have it that I am wronged," I said, "but since we were never formally engaged, I cannot see that I have been. And as for disappointment – well, I faced that long ago. When

William and Georgiana first came to see me after my illness, I could plainly see that he was as far removed from me as the moon. I had stayed still, and he had moved on. I did once think that he loved me, but 'twas only a girlish fancy; a little gallantry, a little charm, and I thought the matter settled! But life is not like that, is it Jenky? And men are not like that. I know that now."

Mrs Jenkinson put her arms around me, and I smelled the old, familiar scent of lavender upon her. For the first time in months, I allowed the tears to spill.

"Oh Jenky," I whispered into her shoulder, "I will have to marry a stranger, or die an old maid. A stranger will only want me for my fortune, and I do not know how I shall bear it. I wish, I wish Papa were here; I wish I could be little Anne again, and not have to face all this."

Mrs Jenkinson stroked my hair, and rocked me as though I were indeed little Anne again. "Shush, shush my chicken," she said, "do not distress yourself so. You are not yet twenty years old; you have all the time in the world. A door has closed, that is all. Another will open in its own good time. There is someone out there for you, my darling - just you wait and see. It will all work out for the best."

I passed the hours as best I could, writing yet again to Georgiana and to Edward to acquaint them with what had happened and prepare them for Mama's displeasure. When she returned, as I knew she would, in high dudgeon at the impudence and selfishness of Miss Bennet, I was even able to draw some amusement from her account of their conversation.

Miss Elizabeth, it transpired, had at first refused either to confirm or deny the existence of an engagement between herself and William.

"Impudent, headstrong girl! She had the effrontery to play tricks with me, repeating my own words back to me - *'Your Ladyship has declared it to be impossible; I do not pretend to possess equal frankness with your Ladyship; if I have drawn him in, I shall be the last person to confess it!'* Insupportable! I reminded her that my nephew was promised to another by the dearest wish of his family; she replied, *'I shall certainly not be kept from marrying him by knowing that his mother and aunt intended him for Miss de Bourgh.'* Yes, she actually said that! She interrupted me at every turn, in the most insolent manner imaginable. She has no shame as regards her family's dubious connections, and when I finally managed to elicit from her the information that she is *not* engaged to my nephew, she refused to give an assurance that she would never enter into such an engagement. Unfeeling, selfish girl! She declared herself determined to act in such a manner as would secure her own happiness, regardless of the consequences for anyone else. I have never met with such brazen insolence in the course of my entire life!"

"They are not engaged?" I repeated slowly, as it dawned on me that matters were not as far advanced as I had supposed; Mama confirmed angrily, "No, they are not – but they might as well be, for all the satisfaction I could get from Darcy!"

"You spoke to William? You saw him? Where? You said you were not going to confront him!"

Mama rapped the chair-arm angrily with her knuckles. "Well I could hardly leave matters as they were, could I? I returned by way of London, and just managed to catch him as he was preparing to leave – another hour, and we would have passed on the road. I demanded an interview there and then, which he could not very well refuse – the expression on his face when he saw me, Anne! Like a cowed, guilty dog! Oh, he knew what I had come for, all right!"

My mind began to race; as Mama recounted, word for word, the exchange that had taken place between herself and William I realised with awful clarity that her intervention must have hastened the very event it sought to oppose. He had been expecting, surely, only to be confronted with his actions in facilitating the marriage of Lydia Bennet to Wickham, assuming that the story had somehow got out; instead, he found himself regaled with Miss Elizabeth's refusal to deny the possibility of an engagement between them and her readiness to accept his declarations with pleasure! Any uncertainty he might have been harbouring regarding her feelings for him would have been well and truly laid to rest by Mama's indignant account of her treatment at Longbourn.

He had said but little, it transpired; but though more reticent than his beloved, he proved equally stubborn. He refused to gainsay Miss Bennet's version of their relationship, or to condemn her rudeness; he declared himself perfectly sensible of what was due to our family, and would not have it that he would be disgracing his relatives in marrying Miss Bennet. He also denied any obligation to me, begging to remind Mama, as I had done numerous times, that no formal engagement had ever existed between us.

I must admit that is cost me a pang to hear this; in spite of myself, I must have been hoping for some kind remembrance, or message of regret. But the damage was done, the chapter was closed, and Mama with her precipitous interference had hastened its completion. There was nothing for it now but to wait, while she raked over the fires of her indignation, for the inevitable announcement of Fitzwilliam Darcy's forthcoming marriage.

*****chapter twenty-five*****

'Longbourn, October 11th

'Dear Lady Catherine,
'I think it best to write to you at once with news which might otherwise reach you from another quarter. Miss Elizabeth Bennet has consented to become my wife, and we will be married here in Hertfordshire next month.
'From the opinions which you expressed at our last meeting, I know that this event will not be welcome to you; but I would beg to remind you, dear Aunt, that I have in no way acted improperly by proposing to Miss Bennet, neither have I broken any promise nor injured any member of my family by engaging myself to a gentlewoman of untarnished reputation.
'I would hope in due course to receive the congratulations and best wishes of all my family upon my marriage, and I would ask to be kindly remembered to my cousin Anne.
'I remain, Madam,
'Your respectful nephew,
'Fitzwilliam Darcy.'

This was the letter that arrived at Rosings within the fortnight, and which Mama thrust indignantly into my hands. Whilst I perused it, drawing what comfort I could from his at least feeling it necessary to mention me, Mama fumed and fretted and vowed that no-one of the name of Darcy would ever again be received under her roof.

"And if he thinks he will be receiving any congratulations from *me,*" she declared, "He is sorely mistaken. I shall write and make it clear that this disgraceful alliance shall never have *my* blessing."

"Would it not be more dignified, Mama," I urged weakly, "not to enter into any correspondence on the subject? We knew that this was going to happen. Can we not just leave them alone?"

"I have every intention of leaving them alone," she replied with asperity, "*When* I have made my position clear. I shall not be denied the opportunity to express myself, Anne. They shall know of my displeasure."

"I think we may safely assume that they know of it already, Mama," I sighed; and she turned on me angrily, saying "There is no call to make clever remarks, Anne; you are partly to blame for all this, you know. You let him slip through your fingers, because you would not give yourself the trouble of fighting for him. And who is going to marry you now?"

This time I was stung into retaliation, speaking with a confidence I was far from feeling: "Since I am still the heiress of Rosings, Mama, I am sure I need not give up all hope of finding a husband just yet;

that is, if you will cease telling everyone that I am engaged to my cousin, which you cannot well help doing now!"

I quitted the room with as much dignity as I could muster, leaving her to give vent to her feelings in a letter to William which I never saw, and to which she never received a reply.

Having severed all connection with the Darcys and intimidated the Collinses into avoiding any mention of Hertfordshire, we received no account of how the wedding went off. Edward's kindly note on the occasion of my twentieth birthday contained no mention of our cousin's nuptials though I knew him to have been among the guests. When Mama announced that she had invited 'the dear Colonel' to spend Christmas with us, I looked forward to satisfying my curiosity on the subject – a curiosity which I knew my mother to share.

He arrived during the third week of December, and we were impressed to hear that he had left a lively family gathering in Hampshire to be with us.

"You are welcome, Fitzwilliam, at this sad time!" was Mama's sombre greeting, as though he had recently attended a funeral rather than a wedding.

He replied soberly, "I am very glad to be here, ma'am. I shall much prefer the peace of Rosings to the chaos I have left behind at Evesham. My nephews and nieces require constant amusement, and they try my father's patience sorely. You have granted me a welcome reprieve!"

Mama made only the briefest inquiries after her brother's health and family, so eager was she to hear Edward's account of the Hertfordshire nuptials. She pressed him for details: how had William conducted himself? What manner of hospitality had Mr and Mrs Bennet provided for their guests? How had the Bennet sisters behaved? Surely the Wickhams had not been invited? She seemed almost disappointed when he confirmed that they had not, though she still found plenty to pass judgment upon. Apparently the two eldest Miss Bennets had been married together at a single ceremony, an economy which Mama thought exceedingly vulgar, though she reflected with satisfaction that Mr and Mrs Bennet had not the resources to supply two wedding breakfasts in as many months. She inquired sourly which bride Edward had thought the better looking, and was pleased to hear him declare in favour of Mrs Bingley. The younger Bennet girls, he reported, had behaved very quietly; indeed they had little chance to behave otherwise, since their mother's volubility dominated every conversation! Mr Bennet, however, was a pleasant, well-mannered gentleman and the hospitality had been generous.

"Well!" declared Mama when her interrogation had run its course, "Charles Bingley has proved himself every bit as foolish as I judged him to be; and as for Darcy, he will now have leisure to reflect upon his rashness, and repent it. Mrs Bennet for a mother-in-law! Well, he has made his bed and will have to lie in it."

"Quite so, ma'am," concurred Edward with the faintest hint of a smile.

"'And now, dear Colonel," she continued in peevish tones, "I have only you to rely on, and I hope you will not disappoint me. Anne's future lies in your hands. I am speaking, of course, of the task of finding her a husband! Since she has no brother, it must fall to you to make the proper introductions. Now, I have thought it all through: do not Mr and Mrs Fitzwilliam go to Bath in the Spring? No doubt they have a large acquaintance there. You must escort Anne thither from Rosings after Easter, to visit her relations and widen her horizons."

I know not who was the more taken aback by these unexpected and precipitate instructions, myself or Edward.

"Dear Mama," I protested, "I do not know whether I shall feel equal to such a journey, or to going into society just yet."

She regarded me scornfully. "You should have though of that, Anne, before letting go of your cousin so readily. I have been too indulgent of you, I see that now. Your constitution has improved beyond anything this last year or two; it is your spirits that want encouragement. You shall go to Bath to take the waters and be introduced to suitable families, with sons. You will see to it, will you not, Fitzwilliam? Though I warn you, I will have no Mortons! Your sister-in-law's relations leave much to be desired in my opinion!"

When Edward and I were alone together I

attempted frantically to dissuade him from my mother's reckless plan, while he tried to reassure me. Bath, he said, was delightful in the Spring, and much less boisterous than London or Brighton. He was sure my cousin Augusta would be a most solicitous chaperone. I would not be besieged by an army of suitors – nothing so indelicate - I would merely be attending a few concerts and dances in pleasant company, with Edward himself at my side.

He then produced a note from Georgiana, which I eagerly devoured. She wrote briefly that she wished our friendship to continue despite the rift caused by her brother's marriage. She was to remain at Pemberley with her brother and sister-in-law when Mrs Annesley returned to London. She hoped that Mama's displeasure would soon abate, and that we would be able to meet before too long.

"This is a kind letter," I said when I had read it, "and I will send her an early reply. There can be nothing to prevent my corresponding with Georgiana."

"I am glad of it, Anne," replied Edward warmly, "for I know that she holds you very dear, as do I."

He reached for my hand with the brotherly affection that had always made his company so welcome to me. "I promised my uncle, as I think I once told you, that I would look after the library, the Park, and the heiress of Rosings for him. Well, I have kept my word as regards the Park and the library, and now that I have my aunt's express charge also I shall do my best to ensure the future happiness of my dearest Anne. Do not distress yourself – if Bath does not produce someone to your liking, we shall take out time and look elsewhere."

He pressed my hand with a smile; I could contain my agitation no longer.

"But I do not *want* to look elsewhere, Edward!" I wailed. "I do not *want* to be forced into marriage with a stranger! I had hoped to make a match *within my own family.* I still do."

It was a speech I been rehearsing in my mind many times over the past fortnight, though I had hoped to deliver it with greater composure. Lying awake at night, scanning the darkness for a chink of light from the door that Mrs Jenkinson had assured me would open in its own good time, I had suddenly remembered William's words: *'Fitzwilliam will be expected to marry at some stage, and he will wish to do it with as little trouble to himself as possible.'*

It was a door, was it not? A dear, familiar door, reluctantly closed in childhood but hopefully not locked. I had determined there and then to try the handle, come what may.

There was a brief, uncomfortable pause following my outburst, and a flush appeared on Edward's cheek. "Well, you are naturally shy of strangers Anne, since you have been so little in company; but strangers become friends given time …"

I remained stubbornly silent, and he continued painfully, letting go my hand, "If it is me you are thinking of, Anne, I am afraid it would not do. I should be a great disappointment to you."

This was the opening I had been waiting for, and I boldly set my foot upon the threshold.

"I do not see how, Edward, since I have no expectations to speak of. I seek only a pleasant companion and a comfortable home. Do you not remember saying to me, when I was quite little, that plenty of people would advise you to marry an heiress, and acquire an estate that way? Well, where would you find a more accommodating heiress, or a pleasanter estate, than right here at Rosings?"

Now it was Edward's turn to remain silent. Tremulous though I was, I pressed home my advantage.

"Mama imagines every woman to have the same expectations as herself, and consequently the same capacity for disappointment. She married poor Papa without knowledge of his nature; that would not be the case with us. I have not her robust constitution, my needs and requirements are different. Edward, I clearly recall your saying only last Spring that the world would be a happier place if we could only accept the fact that people are different."

The expression on my cousin's face was a sight to behold. I knew that I had said enough, that he could not mistake my meaning. At length he passed a hand across his brow, in a gesture reminiscent of Papa; he seemed to collect himself, reached for my hand again, and began to speak quietly.

"Anne," he said, "Do this for me. Come to Bath at Easter, as my aunt has requested. We will take the waters together, we will frequent the Assembly

Rooms, we will meet whomever there is to be met with, and I will bring you home an engaged woman. Whom you choose to engage yourself to shall be up to you – you may count me as one of your suitors, if you wish – but at least it shall never be said that you had no better choice. What say you to that?"

It was not the answer I had been hoping for, but it would do; relief and resignation mingled in my breast as I held my cousin's kind, anxious gaze.

"Will you promise to stay by me, and not leave me too much to cousin Augusta?"

With his free hand, Edward gave a military salute. "I will hardly leave your side."

A smile played about my lips as I slowly nodded my assent.

"Very well then Edward," I said. "I accept your proposal."

*****Epilogue*****

A smile plays about my lips now, as I finish reading the history thus hurriedly concluded. I wrote it, as I recall, in the space of three months, hardly leaving my bureau from January 'til April! Mama, convinced that I was writing a lurid novel, became concerned for my state of mind, repeatedly reminding me that I was going to Bath after Easter and begging me to cease my 'scribbling' and concentrate instead upon preparing for my introduction into society. I paid her little heed. I reasoned that my dress and my manners were already good enough for Edward, and assured her that I felt myself quite equal to the challenge, and that she need not worry about me because my cousin would take care of everything. She looked dubious, and began to talk of coming with us, a possibility that alarmed me greatly until the arrival of the Collins baby provided a reprieve. Convinced that the parish of Hunsford could not do without her at such a time my mother eventually waved me off without demur, approving my calm and cheerful demeanour and pressing Edward's hand warmly as he mounted the carriage steps.

I had planned to take up my pen directly we returned, and finish off my history with a few self-congratulatory sentences; but I found myself too happy, too immersed in my own good fortune, too busy *living* my new life to waste time writing about it. So now, three years later, on the eve of our first visit to Pemberley since the milestone of William's marriage, I am adding a much-needed postscript.

The carriage has been ordered for immediately after breakfast. We will take the barouche, since the weather is unusually fine for May. Mama will sit with her son-in-law, looking forward no doubt to have the Darcys observe him hand her down when we arrive, and I will sit backward with Mrs Jenkinson and Baby; poor Dawson is, as usual, relegated to the box with the driver. I worry about subjecting my cherub to so long a journey, but it would have been churlish to refuse so handsomely worded an invitation and Mama would not countenance anything less than a visit *en famille.*

At any rate, it will be a pleasure to see Georgiana again! When she came here last autumn bearing the Darcy olive branch, she seemed so grown up and confident that I barely recognised the schoolgirl of my former acquaintance ... that visit did much to break the ice with Mama, and to re-establish cordial relations between our two families.

I wonder how William will look, after all this time? Of course Edward has seen him in town, and says he is as handsome as ever, and much more affable in his manner. That will be due to his wife's influence, no doubt; to their conjugal felicity; to the birth of their little daughter. *Anne Elizabeth* – she is named for my aunt, of course, but she is my namesake also. And she is just six months older than little Edward.... but no. I know better than to fall prey to *that* temptation.

I do hope Mama will be civil. I am sure she *intends* to be civil; but I can foresee all descending into criticism and contradiction if Mrs Darcy is not disposed to show deference. And no doubt Elizabeth – *'my cousin Elizabeth'* as Mr Collins would say – is as sharp and vivacious as ever, and knowing all that Mama has said about her she can hardly be kindly disposed towards us ... but it is useless to speculate. They must get along as best they can. I am resolved to be calm and gracious myself, and I will have my husband by my side to support me.

I must not forget to pass on Mrs Collins' compliments to her friend! I called at the Parsonage this morning – little Charlotte was running about the garden with such sturdy confidence! And now they are apparently expecting another – Mr Collins almost bursts at the seams with satisfaction. I wish I could report that fatherhood has rendered him more sensible, but I cannot. Poor Mrs Collins.

I suppose we shall encounter the Bingleys at some point, since they are now established less than thirty miles from Pemberley. However, Edward assures me that Mrs Bingley has 'the sweetest temper in the world', and that we need not dread the introduction. I just hope the Hursts and Miss Caroline will not be in attendance ... but as I said, it is useless to speculate. I shall take all in my stride.

I do wish Edward were coming with us! But he is away with his regiment again, and I cannot complain, for he spends much time at Rosings even though he has a home at Evesham with John and Augusta; my Uncle Fitzwilliam died two years ago, and they are now Lord and Lady Amberleigh.

Dear Edward! He is deserving of all that is good. He is such a devoted godfather – I was right to persuade Frank to break with convention, and name our firstborn son after the one who schemed so cleverly to introduce us.

"Anne, I would like you to meet my dear friend and fellow officer Colonel Charles Bonchurch, younger son of Sir Francis Bonchurch, of Efford Park in Devonshire. He is here with his wife, who is most eager to make your acquaintance! His elder brother is also just arrived in Bath - they will all be attending the concert at the Assembly rooms tonight. Now Anne you promised! *- and I will keep to my part of the bargain, and hardly leave your side..."*

Frank and I will have been married three years in September! And my health has improved so greatly along with my happiness over that time that I am forced to give Mama credit for her diagnosis – the trouble did indeed lie in my spirits rather than my body. Or maybe the waters at Bath really do have miraculous qualities... either way, I am not the listless, pale invalid that once I was. Cousin Elizabeth is in for a surprise in that regard.

My candle is low, and I will not disturb the

servants by ringing for another so late. I shall just look in on little Edward ... no, maybe not, for Mrs Jenkinson was so cross with me for waking him the last time. Dear Jenky – so happy for me, and so pleased to have a third generation of the family placed into her care.

Well I will go to Frank then, for I know he waits up for me. He says he is consumed with curiosity to meet the man who was fool enough to pass me over! But I have told him to treat William kindly, for has he not done us the greatest favour? If he had not closed that door in my face I would never have found, would never have tried, the door to Frank's good heart. I would never have met, or been free to marry, the one man so perfectly suited to my temperament, taste and intellect that I can honestly bless the day that Elizabeth Bennet crossed Fitzwilliam Darcy's path.

Yes, I shall enter the grounds of Pemberley tomorrow with equanimity. I shall even greet Mrs Darcy with affection. The wife of Mr Frank Bonchurch, heir not only to substantial property in Devonshire but also to such a loving and generous nature as is seldom to be met with, has such extraordinary sources of happiness necessarily attached to her situation that she can, upon the whole, have no cause to repine.

****

ACKNOWLEDGEMENTS

Grateful thanks to Magenta Wise and Gregory Nelson, for help and advice patiently given; and to Les, for always believing.

****

Rohase Piercy was born in London in 1958, and now lives in Brighton on the South Coast of England with her husband Leslie and dog Spike. She has two grown-up daughters.

Also by Rohase Piercy

My Dearest Holmes

The Coward Does It With A Kiss

A Case Of Domestic Pilfering

For Children:
What Brave Bulls Do
(Illustrated by Nina Falaise)

Printed in Poland
by Amazon Fulfillment
Poland Sp. z o.o., Wrocław